A Book

For

All Seasons

By

Westcliff-on-Sea Women's Institute
(WoSWI) Writing Group

Published by WoSWI Writing Group

ISBN 978-0-9934063-2-4

Edited by Kim Kimber
(www.kimkimber.co.uk)

With thanks to Trisha Todd (www.ttproofreading.com)
and Sue Duggans for their help with proofreading

Cover image © Connie Larsen
Dreamstime.com

Proceeds from this anthology are being divided between
Southend Mencap Operatic and Dramatic Society
(MODS) and Westcliff-on-Sea Women's Institute
(WoSWI)

Contents

Introduction

I never imagined when I first suggested the idea of a writing group to the then president of Westcliff-on-Sea Women's Institute that we would still be running six years later. But here we are, as enthusiastic as ever, an eclectic mix of old and new members with a shared love of writing.

Our first anthology, *Write On The Coast*, was published in 2013 and in 2015 the group published *Ten Minute Tales*, which won *Writing Magazine*'s Writers' Circle Anthology Award the following year. I am pleased to say that WoSWI Writing Group's list of achievements continues to grow with several members having attained individual success in writing competitions or having had their work published in magazines or online.

For the past few months we have been exploring different genres and in this, our latest anthology, you will find ghostly tales, fantasy, romance, humour and crime. There is something for everyone to dip into during a spare moment. *A Book For All Seasons* has tales set throughout the year so whether you are wrapped up in a blanket on a chilly winter night or basking on a sun lounger sipping a cocktail in radiant sunshine there is a story to suit the occasion.

As with our previous books, the proceeds of this

anthology are being donated to charity, this time shared between Westcliff-on-Sea Women's Institute (WoSWI) and MODS, a drama group for adults with learning difficulties and disabilities. More information about these two organisations can be found at the back of the book.

On behalf of WoSWI Writing Group, I would like to thank everyone who has supported us and our chosen charities by buying our first two anthologies. If you enjoy reading *A Book For All Seasons,* do let us know or post a review on Amazon. Hopefully we can raise lots more money to support worthy causes.

Kim Kimber
(Founder of WoSWI Writing Group)

SPRING

Bubbles

Pat Sibbons

Becky rather liked living above the laundrette. The air always smelt of washing powder and it saved her from trying to squeeze a washing machine into her tiny flat. She would nip down early and nab her favourite machine, the one at the far end, load it and go back upstairs for an hour while her smalls were washing.

This particular spring morning she was trying to decide what to wear for the girls' night out later. *Something sparkly*, she thought.

As she reached into the drum, to deposit her black jeans, her wrists were firmly grabbed. Normally, Becky would have let out a scream and thrashed about but a wave of calm washed over her. Something inside her told her not to be afraid. Whoever had hold of her was now pulling her into the machine.

Surely one of the other customers will grab my legs or raise the alarm, she thought. *The old lady with the annoying cough could at least yell for help.*

But as she began to enter the strangely spacious chasm of the machine no one in the shop seemed to take any notice of Becky's predicament. She was now inside the drum with her dirty clothes.

'I hope that Bolognese stain comes out of my blue blouse,' she said as she travelled past it. As she approached her favourite black top, the drum of the machine seemed to widen into a cave. *Blimey*, thought Becky.

She turned to look behind her to see if a rescue was being attempted but the laundrette had disappeared. Looking forward again, Becky found herself lying on the floor of the cave. Standing in front of her was a middle-aged man dressed in a shabby dinner jacket.

'Did you pull me in here?' asked Becky crossly. 'I need to get my washing sorted. I'm out later and I need to exfoliate.'

'Sorry about that,' said the man. 'We desperately need help so I took the liberty of bringing you here. I'm Hendricks by the way. I already know your name. We have been watching you for a while.'

'Been watching me, have you? I hope you aren't some kind of perv. I wondered where my black lace knickers had gone.'

'I am not a perv, thank you very much, and I certainly have not been anywhere near your undergarments. I am a fairy.'

Becky let out one of her shrieks, saved only for the funniest situations.

'A fairy! Come off it. Fairies look like Tinkerbelle. Pretty little things with wings.'

Hendricks scowled at her.

'That is what Walt Disney would have you believe, but in the real world fairies look like humans, more or less.'

How disappointing, thought Becky and her face must have shown this.

'I do have wings,' he said, turning round to display his back.

'They're a bit small aren't they?' giggled Becky as she looked at two pathetically tiny wings in the middle of Hendricks' back. 'Can you fly with those?'

'Of course not! I weigh thirteen stone. They are more of a symbol these days. Anyway, if we have to go out into the human world we need to be able to tuck them out of sight.'

'Okay, so what do you want with me? Why have you brought me here? I need to get back and sort my laundry out. I've got stuff to do you know.'

'Follow me.'

Hendricks turned and led Becky out of the cave into an enormous tearoom. The tables seemed to go on for miles. At each of the tables sat a group of very glum-looking fairies. The women dressed in tatty, faded summer dresses and the men in shabby suits and dinner jackets. The tables were laid out with a mouldy-looking afternoon tea. The finger sandwiches were dry and curled and the scones were going green.

'Welcome to Fairy Land,' said Hendricks sadly.

'What has happened here?' asked Becky as she

viewed the sad scene before her.

'This, my dear Becky, is the result of a severe shortage of fairy dust.'

'What, the sparkly, glittery stuff you lot sprinkle on things to make magic?'

'Becky, Becky, Becky. Again you have fallen into the Walt Disney trap. Real fairy dust is just that. Dust! In the hands of a fairy it can be used to make magic but here we need it to keep things on an even keel. To keep the sandwiches fresh. To keep our fairy karma in harmony – to keep our fairy shit together so to speak.'

'Right. So where has all the dust gone?'

'Well. Our Fairy Queen has been having a tough time recently. She has reached that age when some women begin to struggle. In her case, this being 1027.

'Added to this, or maybe because of this, she has also developed a bad case of OCD. All reason seems to have gone out of the window and she has virtually eradicated all of the dust in Fairy Land by using a powerful spell. She seems oblivious to the harm this is causing. We have tried to tell her but she just says the place is a mess and she can't stand it. Soon, the afternoon tea will have rotted away and that will be the end of us all.'

'That's awful. So how can I help?'

'You work in an electrical shop, don't you? We have seen your uniform going round and round on a cool wash.'

'Yeah, right, but I still don't see how I can help.'

'We think that if we get her one of your human dust removing machines this may satisfy her need and she will remove the spell.'

'So you want me to get you a vacuum cleaner?'

'Exactly,' said Hendricks, clapping his hands in delight.

'Okay, but–

1. Why don't you just magic her up one?
2. If I get it, who is going to pay for it?
3. How do I get it to her?'

'Well, we don't want to use magic. The Fairy Queen will know straight away if we have had a hand in it. We think the novelty of having one from the human world will please her. We will make sure you are more than adequately recompensed for providing her with the machine and, as for getting it here, it will arrive in the same way you did.'

'So, I am supposed to trust you to pay me for it and I am to shove it in a washing machine.'

'Correct. Fairies are unable to tell lies. If that is all clear you can go back now and get the dust machine as soon as you can.'

In front of Becky's eyes the tearoom changed. It was a bit like when you are a child and spill water all over your painting. When the colours stopped running, she found herself standing in front of her washing machine.

'Barking,' said Becky. She almost believed that it

had been some kind of daydream until she spotted the mouldy old scone next to the washing powder.

That afternoon, Becky popped into work and, using her staff discount, purchased a brand-new vacuum cleaner. If, for any reason, she couldn't get it to Hendricks she would get a refund she told herself.

When she got back to the laundrette she found the machine at the end was free. There was a guy, who looked like a student, sitting engrossed in his mobile three machines down, otherwise it was empty.

Becky opened the door and started to push the huge box into the drum.

It is never going to fit, she thought just as the box slid gently away from her hands.

'Good luck, Hendricks,' Becky yelled into the machine after it.

The student gave her a questioning look and returned to his phone.

Becky made her way up to her flat, thinking, *this is the weirdest day of my life. I am £250 out of pocket and will need a few Porn Star Martinis tonight to get over it.*

The following week, Becky made her way down to the laundrette as usual. The events of the previous week seemed like a dream as she loaded the machine.

Pulling out the detergent drawer she found herself looking at a note and a fabric purse.

The note read:

Dear Becky,

Thank you for providing us with the dust removing machine.

The Fairy Queen is beside herself with delight. She has undone the dust removing spell and is content to just use the machine to clean her palace.

Already the sandwiches and cakes are looking fresher. I am sorry but we don't have any human money to give you, so have given you some of ours.

Best wishes,

Hendricks.

'Bugger,' shouted Becky. 'What am I going to do with fairy money?'

She opened the purse, expecting something resembling Monopoly money and, instead, found it packed with shiny gold coins.

'Thanks, Hendricks,' Becky bellowed into the machine.

'No, thank you, Becky,' echoed back the reply.

Pier Ghosts

Josephine Gibson

It was 9.00am on a cold March morning. Sarah zipped her high-vis jacket to the top of the collar and shook her scraped-back, blonde ponytail, wishing she'd thought to bring a woolly hat.

Yesterday had been fine and sunny – the first day of the year where it had felt like spring – so the fog that now wrapped the seafront was a surprise. There was no wind and the water was barely moving; lacy-edged waves lapped at the shingle almost silently.

As Sarah walked towards the Pier the only sound she could hear was traffic. Her phone buzzed in her pocket and she stopped outside the indoor funfair to read a message. She frowned.

'Typical,' she said to herself and pushed against the glass door of the Pier Entrance, sticking her work-booted foot in the gap as the door was heavy and threatened to swing back on her.

'Help you, miss?' a security man asked, 'We're not open to visitors until ten.'

'Thanks, I'm here on behalf of RJ Surveyors. I think you're expecting me?'

The man raised his eyebrows in surprise and moved behind the counter, pulling out a clipboard with some dog-eared sheets of paper. He ran a thick, dirt-encrusted finger down a column of writing and grunted.

'Well, it says here to expect Mr Roger Jones, Chartered Surveyor.'

Sarah could tell by his expression that he doubted whether a woman of her age and height could be anything to do with surveying and she nodded at him.

'Yes, that's right. I'm Mr Jones's associate. He's just contacted me to confirm that I'll be doing a preliminary visual inspection of the lower decking today and we'll be setting another date shortly to return together to take some samples from the ironwork.'

Sarah pulled her staff pass out from underneath her jacket and hoped she'd sounded convincing. She suspected Roger's sudden 'flu' was self-induced and that he'd be treating it liberally with whisky and lemon. As a junior associate, barely out of university, there was little she could do but cover up, get as much experience as possible and hope to bail out to a better position before Roger's alcoholism became obvious to the powers that be that employed him in the town.

'Is that right?' the man challenged, looking her up and down. 'Well, the Pier trains don't run until ten so you'll have to walk. It's over a mile, you know.'

'Oh, I'm used to that,' Sarah replied, feeling annoyed, 'I'm a local girl. I'll walk this way, shall I?'

She pointed to her left along the platform, 'I'll catch a train on the way back.'

She set off and the man called after her, 'They're only half-hourly, this time of year. Mind you don't miss it; it's a long cold wait for the next one.'

'As if I didn't know,' Sarah seethed picking up her pace. The wooden planks felt moist and as she walked out into the open air the mist enveloped her. Her anger fell away as quickly as it had risen and she squared her shoulders, pulling on the strings of her rucksack to adjust the pack before swinging her arms to establish a walking rhythm. She was lucky, she realised; she could be stuck in an office block in London like many of her friends. Instead, she was out on the iconic landmark of her youth and she felt proud that, in her own small way, she would be able to contribute to its upkeep. Okay, so the 'visual inspection' was unnecessary; Roger had suggested it as a way to save face because he was too hungover to attend the appointment but there was nothing wrong with a walk. It really felt quite special to be walking along the Pier knowing that she was its only occupant.

As she moved away from the coast road, the sound of traffic subsided. Sarah could hear foghorns quite clearly, deep booms from a tanker in the estuary and more high-pitched whistles from a smaller vessel – a fishing boat perhaps? These were the sounds that reminded her of being a child at home, when she'd wake early in the morning and luxuriate in the warmth of bed, knowing from the sounds of the ships that the sea mist had risen. Sarah knew, too, that in a couple of hours the sun would burn through the mist and it would be another beautiful day. The fog was thick here but she imagined a mile inland the sky would already be blue.

Her face felt wet from the fine water droplets in the air and she could see the condensation on the handrails as she walked by. Apart from the foghorns, the crunch of her boots on the planks and the swishing sound of her jacket as she swung her arms, there was no sound. Periodically, she passed a few seagulls poised on the roofs of the shelters built at intervals along the walkway but other than that she was alone. There would be no fishermen at the Pier Head until the first slow train came clanking down the track. Stopping and looking behind her she could no longer see the town, the cliffs or even the two-storey Pier Entrance. It felt like she was marooned on an island.

Sarah shivered a little as she turned back to face the sea, the cold, damp air beginning to penetrate through her clothes. At that moment she felt the Pier move, judder and creak beneath her feet and she heard a crashing sound ahead of her. The seagulls that had been perched placidly around her rose suddenly in alarm, wheeling into the air, crying loudly. What was it? She began to run towards the sound, boots and heart thudding.

Her sudden forward movement caused her left foot to slip behind her on the wet flooring and, before she could stop herself, she was skidding along the ground, arms outstretched, hands and knees abraded by the rough wood. Cursing, Sarah knelt, shaking her wrists to relieve the stinging pain, and looked up.

Her heart skipped a beat. Above her rose the dark hull of a ship. It was so close that Sarah could see water stains on its paintwork. And yet it was eerily quiet and although it sat squarely in front of her – where the Pier should be – the ground felt firm beneath her. Her surveyor's brain told her it could not be so and that she needed to move quickly out of danger. Grabbing her phone, which had slid out of her pocket, she turned and fled, poking at the phone's screen in order to call the emergency services. She couldn't believe it – a vessel had crashed into the Pier right in front of her eyes.

When Sarah reached what she judged to be a safe distance – a couple of stanchions from the accident – she connected to the emergency operator and turned to face the ship, the enormity of the incident impressing on her the responsibility to accurately describe what had happened. 'Hello, Emergency. What service do you require?' the operator asked.

'I, I...' her voice faded. Sarah could not say anything. She disconnected.

A shaft of sunlight broke through the mist and the Pier stretched ahead of her. Empty.

Sarah moved to a bench and sat down, not noticing the dampness. She did not notice the passage of time either, until she felt a hand on her shoulder.

'You alright love? We got a call from the emergency services.' It was the security guy from the front entrance.

'Oh, oh yes,' Sarah replied, 'I fell down, I thought...I thought I'd broken something.' She smiled up at him, her eyes squinting in the sunshine.

'Best come back on the train then, love. I bet your boss won't mind if you leave work for today.' He looked down at her, the heel of her hands scratched and red, a hole in the knee of her jeans. 'Tell you what; you can sit up in the driver's cabin with me. Looks like you had a nasty fall there. You aren't the first though and you won't be the last. All sorts of accidents we have down here – to say nothing of the fires! Tell you what – we've even had a boat sail straight through the Pier. A mile and a half off course it was – wrecked the place! Now, what was it called? There's a photo of it in the Pier Museum – happened in the eighties, I think.'

'It was the MV *Kingsabbey*,' Sarah replied. She had seen its name and would never forget it, glistening, wet, rising above her.

The Birthday

Kim Kimber

'Happy Birthday to you, Happy Birthday to you,' the voices chorus down the phone.

I try to imagine them, Lizzie and her family, gathered round the phone singing but find that I can't quite bring them all to mind. There's too much background noise and I find it hard to think.

'Happy Birthday, Mum,' says Lizzie, after the final flourish. 'I'll be round to pick you up at twelve so remember not to have a sandwich.'

'But I always have a sandwich for my lunch; ham and pickle,' I say.

'I know,' Lizzie sighs and I can picture her face, wrinkled in a frown. 'But not today, we're taking you out, remember?'

'Will there be sandwiches?'

'I don't know, Mum, but it's a lovely place so if they serve sandwiches they will be very nice ones.'

'Can I have ham and pickle?'

'I'm not sure, maybe not today. It's your birthday; it will be good for you to have a change. Don't forget, I'll be round at twelve. Write down the time so that you remember. Mandy is going to help you get dressed.'

Mandy is my carer. I know that; I see her every day. Sometimes I forget her name – I forget a lot of things these days, especially names – but Mandy has a lovely, kind face and I am always pleased to see her. I look down; I am dressed already, so that means Maddie, I think that's her name, has already been in. She comes every morning to help me get washed and get into my clothes as I find the fastenings fiddly. I appear to be wearing rather a smart skirt for indoors but then maybe my other ones are in the wash. Lizzie does all my washing these days. I must make a note to ask her.

I reach for my notebook and write down 'skirt' and next to that 'Lizzie'. Thinking of my daughter, I recall that she also asked me to note something down, but I can't remember now. It was something about lunch and a sandwich but it's gone from my mind so I draw a sandwich and a smiley face, the way my grandson, Luke, has shown me how to when something makes me happy. He's a good boy, Luke. Being with him gives me a warm feeling, a bit like cake or a ham and pickle sandwich.

The morning passes slowly. I read a chapter of my book, a new crime thriller by my favourite author, or at least so Lizzie tells me. I seem to have been reading it for a very long time and am no nearer to finding out who committed the crime. In fact, it all feels very familiar, as if I have read this book before.

Bored with reading, I turn on the TV and start to watch a programme about baking. The lady on the screen is covering a gooey orange cake with dark chocolate. It looks delicious, I do like cake. My grandson, Luke, bakes. My son-in-law – what is his name? Anyway, he doesn't approve but Luke makes wonderful cakes and wants to go to catering school. His dad – I can't seem to remember his name – wants him to go into insurance like himself but I think Luke should make cakes if he wants to. Everyone likes cake; it makes people happy.

All those cakes on the TV make me hungry. I look at the clock – eleven thirty, too early for lunch. But I am hungry so I go into the kitchen expecting to see my sandwich already prepared and waiting for me. It's not there and I am sure that I haven't eaten it already. I am definitely hungry, maybe Millie forgot. Never mind, I can make it myself. I fancy ham and pickle, yes, that will make a nice change. Very carefully, I remove two slices of bread from the package, smother them with butter and add two slices of ham. The final touch is a lovely dollop of old-fashioned, sweet brown pickle. It takes me a long time but, eventually, I carry my sandwich on a plate back to the lounge and settle in my chair.

It tastes wonderful. *I should have this every day*, I think to myself. I am just finishing the last mouthful when Lizzie bursts through the door, looking flustered.

Lizzie is my eldest child and only daughter, and she is always flustered.

'Mum,' she shrieks, 'what are you doing?'

'Eating my sandwich,' I say, 'ham and pickle; you should try it.'

'No, Mum, we're going out to lunch today, it's your birthday, remember?'

I look at the cards that Mollie has arranged on the mantelpiece and smile. Of course, how lovely. 'Does that mean that I can have cake?' I ask, smiling.

'Yes, later, but first we are going out to lunch. Everyone is waiting for you at that new café along the seafront. I've come to pick you up.'

'I know that,' I say, 'I'm wearing my going out skirt.'

Lizzie helps me to put on my outdoor shoes and bundles me into my coat. She looks cross.

'We're late and you've already eaten. You don't know how hard it was to get a booking.'

'Let's go then,' I say, 'Chop, chop.'

The restaurant is busy and Lizzie steers me, a little roughly I feel, to a table in the corner where several people I recognise, but can't quite put a name to, kiss me on the cheek.

Cards, flowers and boxes of chocolates are thrust into my hands and I feel the familiar anxiety creep over me.

'Where am I?' I ask.

'It's okay, Nan,' says a voice I recognise, as Luke takes my hand. He is such a lovely boy and handsome too. At seventeen, he stands well over six feet tall and has wonderful waves of ebony curls. He reminds me of his grandfather. The thought of my husband makes me feel sad and a tear escapes down my face. How proud he would have been of them all if he hadn't been taken too soon by that cruel disease, cancer.

'We're all here,' soothes Luke, not letting go of my hand, 'and I'm going to sit right beside you.'

I look around the table and concentrate very hard. The mass of faces begin to take on their individual identities. There are Lizzie's twin daughters, Sophie and Megan, who are both staring at their phone screens, my son-in-law, whose name I still can't remember, James, Jack, no Jeremy, that's it, I smile triumphantly to myself, the same as that man who drives cars on the TV and is always in trouble. Then there is Lizzie, of course, whose face is now red and sweaty. Lastly, there is my son, Michael, who is holding the hand of a young lady I don't recognise.

'Who's that?' I whisper to Luke, pointing towards the woman.

Luke laughs, 'That's Charlie, Uncle Mike's girlfriend, you've met her before, Nan.'

I study Charlie. Long blonde hair, heavy make-up, too-tight top, no I am sure that I would have remembered. I am about to ask what happened to

Michael's wife when the waitress arrives to take our order.

'Birthday girl first,' says Luke. 'What would you like, Nan?'

'Ham and pickle,' I say, wondering why I don't feel hungry.

The waitress looks blank.

'Would it be possible to make a ham and pickle sandwich?' asks Luke. 'It's my nan's favourite.'

'What kind of bread do you want?' asks the waitress, 'wholemeal, granary, gluten-free, panini?'

'Can't I just have Hovis?' I say in bewilderment.

Luke steps in. 'Wholemeal will be fine,' he says with his dazzling smile and the waitress fiddles with her hair and suddenly becomes a lot more interested in our order.

A short while later, the food arrives and I am presented with a doorstep of a sandwich with thick ham and homemade chutney, not pickle, I notice. It is covered with a blanket of green leaves, which taste strange and peppery and is not like any lettuce I have had before. I spit it out into my serviette, hoping no one will notice but they are all too busy chatting. They talk too fast and I can't keep up with most of what is said but I am happy to be with them. I fiddle with my sandwich, rearranging it on the plate.

'It's okay to leave it, Nan,' says Luke, patting my hand.

The waitress arrives and removes my plate. 'Didn't you like your sandwich?' she asks me but smiling at Luke.

'Not really, the ham was too thick, it wasn't pickle and the lettuce tasted funny.'

'It's rocket,' she says, her eyes still fixed on my grandson.

Luke returns the waitress's smile, leans across and whispers in her ear and she disappears back into the kitchen. I look across at Lizzie, who is wearing a serious expression and talking through the side of her mouth to Jason, or is it John, I never can remember. Neither of them looks very happy.

Just then the waitress returns with a cake with lots of flaming candles and there is a round of 'Happy Birthday'. I didn't realise that it was someone's birthday; that must be why we are having a special lunch. I hope I got them a present. I join in with the singing until the waitress puts the cake in front of me. Then I remember.

'Blow them out, Nan,' encourages Luke. I take a deep breath but I don't seem to have as much puff as I used to and it takes several goes before all the candles are out. The cake looks delicious, covered in a rich, dark chocolate.

'I made it for you, Nan,' says Luke, 'chocolate sponge with a chocolate ganache.' It does look lovely and I do like cake – but I am sure that I have had that cake already today – it looks very familiar and I'm really not very hungry.

'We'll box it up for you,' says Luke, as if he can read my thoughts. 'You can have some at home later.'

And that's what I do. The cake is delicious with a rich, creamy centre. I share it with Mindy who has come to help me get ready for bed. She is a lovely girl, always smiling.

'This is really good,' she says, with her mouth full.

'My grandson made it,' I say, feeling pleased. 'We had lunch.'

'That's right,' says Mandy, 'for your birthday. What did you have? I bet it was something nice.'

I try to remember but my head feels cloudy. Images flash before my eyes but they are fragmented and disjointed like pieces of a jigsaw puzzle and I can't quite fit them together.

'It doesn't matter,' says Mandy, smiling. 'Tomorrow, I'll make your favourite for you, ham and pickle.'

Mother's Day

Lois Maulkin

'Don't you want your gloves on, Mum?' They lay on the sideboard, pressed together, fawn-coloured, neat. A very thin prayer. Looking at them I thought of small, wild animals, hibernating, warm belly to warm belly in silent, dreamless companionship.

'No, thank you,' she said, buttoning up her coat. 'We'll be in the car, won't we?'

'Yes,' I said, 'but shall I bring them along? If we're going to Westonbirt afterwards...'

She looked sharply at me. 'I shan't be going to Westonbirt. I'll want to come back here afterwards.' She double locked the front door and her best shoes clacked down the path. The gate latch clicked.

I took the direct route out of town and reached the motorway before nine thirty. 'We're okay for time, aren't we?' I asked, to break the silence.

'My appointment is at eleven,' said Mum, sitting back in her seat. We drove on.

'Look, primroses!' I said.

'What, dear?'

'Primroses. On the central reservation; they're your

favourites.'

She looked at me again. 'I'm not senile, you know.'

'I know, Mum. But, well, it's just strange that of all the nice places I could be taking you for Mother's Day, you want to go to this...this...backstreet hairdressers no one's ever heard of, in a town that's fifty miles away. I mean, Westonbirt's lovely this time of year. You love it there. We always go to Westonbirt on Mother's Day.'

'You said I could pick anywhere I liked,' she replied matter-of-factly.

I sighed. 'I know. But why this? Your hair doesn't even need doing. You can get a Sunday appointment with Sheila at Snippets. You always get a lovely cut at Snippets. Has Sheila upset you?'

'No, Sheila has not upset me,' Mum replied. She closed her eyes and, with them, the subject.

I drove on, wondering why it made me feel so uneasy, not knowing Mum's reasons, her whys. Usually, I simply just knew. I knew why she liked a cup with a white inside – so the tea looked a nice tea colour against it. I knew why she never ate strawberries – because, as a child, she'd accidentally bitten into a small slug attached to one. I knew why we had never seen her cry all these years since Dad went – because she knew that if she started she would never stop.

I found the place and we waited in the car until five to the hour. Mum took a deep breath as she unclipped her seat belt. That old-fashioned smell of perm lotion

28

and cooked hair washed over us as we went in.

'I've an eleven o'clock appointment with Hester,' my mother said to the girl at the desk, and gave a false name. My surprise must have shown on my face and I opened my mouth to say something but Mum silenced me with a grim look.

A woman in a red blouse came out of a back room and said to Mum, 'Hello, I'm Hester. Can I take your coat?'

'You'll have to speak up. I'm afraid I'm rather deaf,' said Mum taking her coat off slowly and handing it to the hairdresser who hung it on a peg.

'About this loud?' said Hester chirpily with a little more volume.

I was mystified. This was the first I'd heard about anything being wrong with my mother's hearing.

Hester showed Mum to a seat, a dark throne in front of the merciless mirror, and tied a black nylon cape around her neck.

'That's far too tight,' shouted my mother, flailing about in the chair, 'you're choking me.'

I started up from the plastic sofa and the women in seats on either side of Mum slid their eyes across to look.

'I'm so sorry,' gasped Hester, looking puzzled and adjusting the tapes. I sat down again. The eyes slid back.

'So, what shall we do with you today?' asked Hester to my mother's reflection.

'Pardon?' bawled Mum.

Hester repeated her question more loudly. 'Just a trim. A dry cut. Half an inch,' yelled Mum. I saw her staring through narrowed eyes into the mirror at the hairdresser's face as the plastic comb swept briskly through her dust-coloured strands.

My mother took the conversational lead. 'Going somewhere nice on holiday this year?' she yelled.

'Venice. We go every year,' replied Hester loudly, pulling Mum's hair up in a small sheet between her fingers and snipping along.

'With your family?' hollered Mum.

'No,' smiled Hester, 'just me and my husband.'

Snip, snip, snip.

'Been together long?'

'Seven years now.'

Snip, snip, snip.

'Second time around, was it? I mean, you're no spring chicken are you?' bellowed my mother. I felt hot with embarrassment. One of the other customers tittered and hushed herself quickly.

There was a moment's pause and Hester said, 'Yes, well, no, well, it was the first time for me, anyway,' and raked on through the dry straw of my mother's coiffure.

Snip, snip, snip.

'How old are you?' boomed my mother. 'Sixty? Sixty-five?'

Hester said, 'I'm forty-seven,' and carried on

snipping, trying to catch the eye of the stylist next to her for moral support.

'And how old is he? Bit older than you?'

'A few years, yes.'

Hester snipped on uninterrupted for a few moments, and then Mum said, 'Leave his wife and children for you, did he?'

'I beg your pardon?' said Hester icily, stepping back from the chair. There was a collective intake of breath.

'Just making conversation,' bawled my mother. 'How's my hair looking? Finished, are you?'

'Nearly,' said the hairdresser, visibly pulling herself together and recommencing.

As the comb touched her head my mother screamed so loudly that someone dropped a hairdryer and a woman had her ear snipped. All eyes turned to Hester and my mum. I leapt to my feet.

'You've really, really hurt me,' Mum shouted.

'Sorry,' said Hester, 'I didn't mean to.'

'Pardon?' said my mother. 'Speak up please.'

'Sorry!'

'Louder please.'

'I'M SORRY,' yelled Hester.

The other customers, the hairdressers, the girl on the desk and I sat stunned and staring as my mother rose majestically from the chair, a comb stuck in her hair, and hissed, 'I don't accept your apology, Hester. I don't think you're sorry at all.'

She pulled the comb out and placed it carefully on the side. 'My coat, please.'

Hester, white faced, held the coat out for my mother to put on. Mum shot her arm in through the sleeve and punched Hester squarely and forcefully in the stomach, knocking her backwards across the coffee table and leaving her gasping amongst the magazines.

'Come along, dear,' called Mum as she clacked towards the door. 'If you've brought my gloves, I think I do fancy Westonbirt. After all, it is Mother's Day.'

The Spinsters

Sue Duggans

The sun was slipping towards the horizon, painting the sky orangey-pink, as Ethel, Gladys and Betty slowly climbed the steps to the hotel. The breeze lifted the hem of Ethel's bottle-green dress, revealing her lace-edged petticoat, and she tried to hold it down. The three laughed youthfully.

The ladies met up every two months or so, usually for coffee or lunch, but today was extra-special – afternoon tea at the local boutique hotel. Betty's two nieces had arranged the treat for their aunt and her friends sensing that they missed out every year on Mother's Day celebrations. It was a thoughtful gesture.

Age had been kind to Betty and she'd escaped the curse of arthritis which affected her friends in varying degrees. As they made their way up the steep steps Ethel clung on to Betty who felt vaguely irritated by the slow progress of the other two.

The warm and fragrant welcome of the classy hotel was pleasant. Arrangements of spring flowers, left over from the previous day's Mothering Sunday celebrations, adorned the reception area and lounge. The women were directed towards the restaurant and, slowly but steadily, made their way there. They passed a group of men, young by their measure, who were talking in loud voices and drinking beer. Betty remembered reading in the local paper that golf club members were using the hotel facilities while their clubhouse was undergoing extensive refurbishment. She tutted.

When they finally reached the restaurant, the ladies were greeted by a smiling, attentive and smartly-dressed young girl.

'Hello, ladies. I'm Lucy and I'll be looking after you this afternoon,' she said cordially.

Lucy showed them to a table looking out across the estuary and took their coats. She left them admiring the pink linen napkins, silver cutlery and white china. A little bowl of white and brown sugar cubes and small pots of jam were placed in the middle of the beautifully-arranged table.

Ethel opened the conversation. 'Well, this is very nice. I always look through the window when I go past on the bus. Never thought I'd be sitting here.'

'Fancy!' said Gladys.

Betty smiled a watery smile.

Lucy came back to the table and asked what sort of tea the ladies would like. Ethel's little feet shuffled nervously under the table. *What sort of tea? The brown, hot, sweet type*, she thought. *What sort of question was that?*

'Earl Grey for me, please,' Betty requested.

Ethel felt her cheeks flush beneath her generously-applied foundation. Gladys ordered coffee.

'Just ordinary tea for me, please,' said Ethel quietly. Lucy smiled.

In no time the young waitress returned with two pots of tea and a pot of coffee for Gladys. Behind her a young man carried two trays of neat sandwiches – rectangles cut with precision, the crusts removed.

'What a *wonderful* spread!' remarked Betty.

'Fancy!' said Gladys.

The ladies selected a couple of sandwiches each from the trays and began eating. Betty dusted the crumbs from her mouth and poured her tea.

Ethel was feeling a little nervous in the grand setting and took very small bites from the sandwiches. A globule of creamy egg filling oozed from one and landed on her dress. She took the pink napkin and wiped the mess leaving a visible smear across her chest. She could sense Betty eyeing her disapprovingly and felt the flush return to her cheeks.

After some time Lucy reappeared, this time carrying a cake stand laden with scones and luxurious cakes. Pastries dusted with icing sugar, little tartlets decorated with fresh strawberries and individual Victoria sandwich cakes were arranged perfectly on doilies.

Ethel poured some tea and carefully chose a miniature pastry with nothing gooey which could escape and further garnish her clothing. Gladys tucked in and managed to demolish two scone halves, a pastry and two tartlets.

'I do love cakes,' Gladys stated in a voice rather too loud for the occasion. A small moustache of cream had appeared on her upper lip. This time she was the target for Betty's disapproving looks. Ethel remained oblivious.

'Tuck in, Ethel. You've hardly eaten a thing.' Betty edged the cake stand towards her so she played safe and helped herself to another of the delicate little pastries.

Lucy appeared again. 'How are we doing, ladies?' she asked.

'Oh, I'm having a lovely time, dear,' said Ethel with sincerity. 'We're very good friends, us three, and we meet up quite often. We worked together when we were young, you know, in the big factory, making radios. We had some fun in those days, didn't we, girls?'

Ethel stopped abruptly. Mention of 'the big factory' had produced another of Betty's glares. She was a social climber and had spent much of her adult life shaking off the humiliation of having been a factory girl.

'How interesting! I'm so pleased that you've enjoyed your tea,' said Lucy sweetly. She'd noted 'the glare' and felt embarrassed for this sweet, elderly lady whose face, not for the first time, was flushed.

A sudden, loud roar of laughter could be heard from the lounge bar followed by an expletive-laden exchange from the men and Lucy moved off hurriedly.

Ethel lowered her eyes and her feet began to swing to and fro. It was clear that Betty was far from amused.

'Fancy!' whispered Gladys.

'I need to go to the ladies' room then we'll be off,' Betty announced.

She was gone for some time and Ethel and Gladys chatted while the setting sun cast rose tints across the room. Unexpectedly, their conversation was interrupted by shrieks of laughter and a series of loud whoops and wolf-whistles from the bar. One of the young waitresses must have caught the eye of the men drinking there. How embarrassing for her!

Ethel and Gladys looked in the direction of the racket and saw Betty heading back. Despite her insecurities, Ethel was a perceptive woman but had never before observed the haughty manner which she saw in Betty as she approached. When she sat down at the table Ethel noticed Lucy and the nice young man look in their direction. The young man appeared to be stifling a grin and Lucy whispered in his ear. She came over and stood close to Betty, speaking to her in hushed tones. Her face turned to stone.

'Thank you,' was her expressionless response to whatever it was that Lucy had said. 'We'll be leaving now. Please fetch our coats.'

There were no 'ifs or buts' and Ethel and Gladys took this as their cue to prepare to leave. They slowly got to their feet, wondering what had been said to their friend but all was revealed as Betty rose gradually from her chair. It seemed that everyone in the room was staring at her. In an attempt to be sensitive Ethel tried in vain to look away while Gladys stood with her mouth wide open.

Betty's chiffony, afternoon-tea dress had been well and truly caught in the waist of her knickers revealing voluminous pink pants. As discreetly as she could, but this was extremely difficult, she pulled at her dress tutting all the while. Ethel and Gladys looked on, riveted to the spot, not daring to speak or offer a helping hand. When finished with tugging and tutting, Betty turned away from the other two, smoothing her dress as she did so, then back again and they both nodded in silent approval. Lucy helped them into their coats and the trio headed for the exit. This time Ethel wasn't offered Betty's arm for support.

As the three passed the bar, the men became hushed and fixed their gaze on the women. Betty hurried on ahead followed at a slower pace by Ethel and Gladys. As Betty reached the door, and her escape, one of the men shouted out. 'Nice knickers, love.' Laughter could once again be heard.

'Fancy! Fancy!' said Gladys.

Ethel lowered her head and walked as fast as her arthritic knees and hip would allow.

Betty was mortified and felt short of breath. She

stopped on the top step until her friends caught up. Ethel sensed her fury and said nothing but offered her arm which Betty gratefully accepted. The three stood shoulder to shoulder looking out to sea.

The egg stain, clearly visible on Ethel's dress, would come out in the wash, but for Betty, the memory of her humiliation would take much longer to erase.

The Gift

Barbara Sleap

Gina was preparing food for her youngest daughter Tilly's sixth birthday party. It was also Easter Monday so that was the theme and an Easter bonnet parade and egg hunt were to be included in the celebrations.

As well as family, Gina had invited ten of Tilly's classmates, a lot to cater for. Tilly was already excited and was expectantly watching for her friends to arrive. Gina had hidden coloured plastic eggs around the garden, along with some small furry chicks for the girls, and small yellow footballs for the boys. *Much better than sweets*, thought Gina. She hummed as she prepared chicken nuggets and pizza for the children and quiche and salad for the adults. Thank goodness the weather looked calm, with a milky sun peeping behind wispy white clouds promising to warm the April day.

The kitchen door opened suddenly as Gina's eldest daughter, Katie, flounced into the room, her pink, heart-covered robe wrapped carelessly around her slim frame. She slumped moodily on to a stool.

'Morning dear,' Gina said light-heartedly.

'I don't know why I can't go to Lakeside with Lucy

and Fiona,' Katie whined, 'just because it's Tilly's birthday. I've been swotting all week and worked at the café all weekend. It's bank holiday and my only day off. I need some fun you know. Why have I got to stay here to be smiley and nice to everyone and play stupid games with children?'

'Oh, Katie, just this once, I really need you to help me out. Paul is working until later and everyone will be here soon. Besides, you haven't seen your dad or Nanny, Grandpops, Granma and Grumpy for a while now.'

'For God's sake, Mum, you know I don't use those silly names anymore, it's so childish. I'll be eighteen in a couple of weeks.' Katie took an angry bite of her Marmite-covered toast, before continuing. 'Anyway, Tilly won't care if I'm here or not and you know I can't stand Joyce and Tom's grandkids or Dad's two spoilt brats.'

'Katie, they are not spoilt, they're lovely boys. Please, it would be helpful if you could just give me a hand with the games and music.' Gina looked at her daughter's downcast face. 'Look, the magician is coming at three, Paul will be back, lunch will be over; couldn't you just stay until then?'

Katie's only reply was a deep groan, but Gina persisted. 'Why don't you ask Fiona and Lucy here? You can all have a bite to eat and then go out later; they might enjoy it.'

Katie pouted, 'You must be joking; we were going

to Pancho's.'

'Well, I think you should stay and see your dad and grandparents. They're all eager to hear about your plans for Uni.'

Katie's face softened slightly at the mention of her dad.

'Huh, it's just that I can't stand the way he and Kathy moon all over each other, yuk, it's sickening. I don't know why you want them here, Tilly is nothing to them.'

'Kathy's really nice, Katie, and I'm glad that they're happy. They both adore Tilly and Kathy thinks the world of you, too, if you could just open your eyes. Anyway, they've been invited and that's that.'

Katie pulled a face. 'I just want to spend time with my friends, that's all. We need a break from studying.' She slammed her plate down.

'No more toast then.' Gina tried a smile but Katie was in full flow.

'Besides, Tilly's not even my real sister is she? I'm just the outsider.'

Gina looked up, a hurt expression on her face.

'Outsider? You can't mean that, Katie, Tilly absolutely adores you. I can't believe you said that.'

'Well, that's how I feel. There's you, Paul and Tilly, Dad, Kathy and the twins, then there's me.'

And with that, Katie stamped from the room, slamming the door behind her. After a while loud music emanated from upstairs.

Gina felt shaken by Katie's outburst. She and Dave's divorce had been amicable and they had remained friends. Two years later, she had married Paul and had Tilly. Dave had married Kathy and had the twins soon after. Katie never seemed to mind babysitting the twins and didn't complain about picking Tilly up from nursery, and now school, from time to time. Something must be wrong though. Disconcertedly, Gina reached for the kettle.

The music stopped, suddenly, and Katie reappeared wearing jeans and a brightly coloured top. 'I'm not dressing up,' she remarked bitterly.

'You always look lovely, dear.'

Gina took a long look at her daughter and saw a tall, slight girl with thick, fair hair and realised that Katie was actually quite a stunner. Maybe she had been too busy to notice her daughter change from a child to a young woman; busy with her demanding job, busy with Tilly and working around Paul's relentless shifts. There just never seemed to be enough time.

'Sorry, Mum,' Katie said sheepishly, 'I just wanted to have some fun today.'

Gina eyed her daughter. 'Lives move on, Katie, you'll realise that when you're older. You're lucky that your dad and I aren't always arguing. I mean, look at Lucy's parents, always fighting over something, always at the solicitor demanding money for this and for that.'

'Well, at least they don't make Lucy help at baby parties and have to eat egg sandwiches and chicken nuggets.'

Gina watched as Katie strutted out, talking under her breath as, once more, she made for her room to take solace in music.

The day wore on and was a success; the egg hunt went without argument. Katie picked the winner of the hat parade. The children gasped as the magician wowed them (and the adults) with his tricks. Tilly blew out the candles on her Cinderella cake and, at last, parents arrived to pick up their little darlings. Coats and shoes were frantically searched for and slices of cake, wrapped in serviettes, were handed out.

Katie had had enough. She had dutifully helped with the music for musical statues and pass the parcel, handed out plates of food, poured apple juice and lemonade and mingled with her relatives. Secretly, she had enjoyed telling her grandparents about the university courses she was applying for, and they beamed proudly when they discovered her ambition to be a journalist.

Back in the quietness of her room, Katie sat on the bed. She hadn't wanted to upset her mum but she was tired of being at the beck and call of her parents, babysitting, picking up Tilly, putting Tilly to bed, helping the twins with their reading, on and on. 'Oh, Katie, could you just–'

Katie couldn't wait to get away. Her family didn't

seem interested in her and how she felt. OMG! She didn't even get the Ferrero Rocher Easter egg she'd been hinting about. Her eyes brimmed with frustrated tears just as her phone beeped and she looked at the WhatsApp selfie of Lucy and Fiona holding up their cocktails in Pancho's. That hurt; they could have waited for her, couldn't they?

She looked at the little, pearl-handled penknife laying on her dressing table and stared unhappily at her tear-stained face in the mirror. Could she do it? Several girls at college had and seemed proud of the little angry red scars hidden on their wrists. They said it made them feel important. Katie pulled up her sleeve with determination.

Downstairs all was quiet with just family remaining. Tilly and the boys were playing with her new Swingball and the adults were enjoying a cup of tea with their cake. Gina nodded at Paul and he left the room. He returned with a large bag containing the gold Ferrero Rocher egg and passed it to Dave who slid the key and chain for the little blue Fiat 500 into the box.

'Shall we call her down then?'

Nods of approval were given. They had all contributed to this gift and wanted Katie to have it before her first driving lesson booked on her birthday. *She will love it*, thought Gina, climbing the stairs.

Katie sat staring at the knife poised over her left arm. Did she really need to go to this extreme to make her family understand? Would it hurt? Would it bleed a lot? Tears rolled as the blade touched her skin, making her shudder. At that moment, there was a tap on the door.

'Katie, can you pop downstairs for a minute, we've got something to tell you.'

Guiltily, Katie pushed the little weapon back into the drawer with a feeling of relief. Maybe things weren't *that* bad. What did they want now? OMG! It'd better not be another baby on the way.

Mirror, Mirror

Trisha Todd

'Are you picking up the keys today?' Cheryl laughed as Kelly swung round on her seat to face her, eyes wide and with a beaming smile on her face.

'Yes. I'm so excited!' she squealed.

'I'd never have guessed,' giggled Cheryl, as Kelly did a little jig in her chair.

'I've not had my own place before and I can't wait. No little sister nicking my clothes and make-up, and no parents watching my every move – heaven.'

'Little sister! She's 23!'

'Yes, well, that doesn't stop her, and Mum and Dad still think I'm ten so I'll prove to them that I'm a big girl now.'

At one o'clock, Kelly shut her computer down and gathered up her coat and bag. 'See you tomorrow, Cheryl,' she called as she left the office and rushed to the letting agent in town.

With the keys gripped tightly in her hand, Kelly walked the ten minutes to her new home. It was ideal for her, just twenty minutes from the insurance office where she had worked for the last three years. It had one bedroom that overlooked the garden, belonging to the flat downstairs, a neat little kitchen and bathroom, and a living room with a Juliet balcony so she would be able to throw the doors open in the summer heat, if they got any.

She reached a little charity shop and something glinted in the spring sunshine as she passed, catching her eye. Although she wanted to get to her flat as soon as she could, she felt compelled to stop. There, resting against an old wooden dresser, was a pretty antique mirror, its silver frame shining. A feeling of longing overcame her; she had to have that mirror. *That'll look lovely in my flat*, she thought, as she pushed through the flaking blue door into the dim interior.

'Oh, be careful with this,' huffed the volunteer as she lifted it from the display, 'it's heavier than it looks.' Kelly smiled as she paid the woman and clutched her parcel to her. 'I see what you mean,' Kelly said as she made her way out of the shop.

Kelly put her key into the lock and opened the door to her new life. She sighed happily as she wandered from room to room. *Small but perfectly formed*, she thought as she opened the windows to let in the cool fresh air. Her parents would be round soon with some of her belongings, and she just knew her mum would have enough food with her to stock the kitchen twice over.

Kelly was right. It took a couple of hours to get everything sorted, to make her bed and stow her possessions. Luckily her dad had brought his tool box with him, and had hung the mirror in the bedroom for her while she and her mum made tea.

'Oh, I'm not sure of that,' her mum said when she saw the mirror on the wall. 'It's a bit old-fashioned for you, isn't it? And what's–' she glanced again at her reflection, then shook her head.

'Well, I like it, and it's my place,' Kelly smiled as she handed her parents some biscuits.

Now, finally, she was on her own. 'I think I'll get to bed,' she muttered to herself, and strode into the bedroom to pull the curtains. She stopped suddenly. It was cold, her breath misting in the air and a shiver ran up her spine. Kelly looked to the window but she could see that it was shut. *How odd,* she thought, pulling the curtains, but her neck began to prickle and she felt she was being watched. Her heart thumped in her chest as she turned back to the empty room. As she did, she glanced at the mirror and thought she saw a shadow cross the glass but the feeling soon disappeared and the room was warm once again.

Kelly checked the flat, but her doors and windows were all closed, so she shrugged and put it down to first-night nerves.

She picked up her hairbrush and stood in front of the mirror. *Oh, what's that?* she thought. *I've not noticed that before.* She peered closer at the writing etched within the pattern that wound around the frame.

'When thou lay thee down to sleep,
Pray the Lord thy soul to keep
'Tis Devil's work, without detection,
Thy soul to keep within reflection.'

'Hmm,' she said to herself in the mirror. 'That's not the prayer I remember.' She turned to switch off the light and got into bed, not noticing the eyes still staring at her from the silvered glass.

Through the night, Kelly tossed and turned in bed. She woke with a start to find the covers twisted around her legs and she sat up to turn on her bedside lamp. *Just a nightmare*, she told herself but the feeling of being watched had returned. 'For God's sake, Kelly,' she whispered angrily. 'Get a grip!' but as she lay back down she didn't see the shadow move across the mirror once more.

At work the following day, Cheryl commented on the dark circles under her friend's eyes. 'Late night?'

'Ah, yes, kind of,' Kelly yawned. 'Had a nightmare and couldn't get back to sleep. Not used to being on my own I suppose.' For the next few days, though, Kelly woke with a splitting headache and she felt a bit shaky.

'I think you need to get your boiler checked,' Cheryl suggested. 'Perhaps it's leaking carbon monoxide or whatever. And eat more, you're losing weight!'

The check revealed nothing wrong with the boiler so Kelly put her headaches down to not sleeping properly and being extra busy at work, but she caught Cheryl looking worriedly at her a couple of times. It was with relief that Friday night arrived and Kelly could have a couple of days to sleep late if she wanted. Head still thumping, she stood in front of her mirror, brushing her hair, when she thought her reflection wavered. She peered closer and for just a moment, the eyes that stared back did not look like hers. *You're going mad, girl,* she thought. *Either that or it's a migraine and I'm seeing things.* Resolving to make an appointment with the doctor if she didn't feel better by Monday, Kelly got into bed and turned off the light.

As she fell into a fitful sleep, the temperature in the room plummeted, and Kelly began to moan. In the darkness, she wouldn't have been able to see the hungry eyes that watched her or the shadow that detached itself from the mirror and hovered once again over her prone form. As Kelly exhaled her misty breath, it was sucked into the darkness that lay over her.

When Kelly eventually staggered out of bed the next morning, she was shocked at her reflection in the mirror. Her usually shiny blonde hair hung limply around her gaunt, pale face and her half-lidded eyes were dull and sunken above dark shadows. She turned and went straight back to bed.

Cheryl wasn't surprised when Kelly didn't arrive for work on Monday although it was a little strange that she hadn't called to let Jackie, their manager, know she was sick. 'I'll call round in my lunch break,' she decided.

As she rounded the corner into Kelly's road, Cheryl was greeted by the blue lights of an ambulance and a police car and she ran to Kelly's door, not noticing the black coroner's car parked further along the road.

'What's happened?' she shouted at a young paramedic in a green uniform. There was movement at the door, and she saw Kelly's mother, supported by a policewoman, walk out ahead of a stretcher. The red blanket completely covered the body underneath.

Cheryl gasped and Kelly's mother looked up, showing the tears that ran unchecked over her pale, blotchy face. 'Oh Cheryl, she's gone. My Kelly's gone!'

There was a police investigation and an inquest but no cause of death could be found. Although the coroner could not explain how it had happened so quickly, it seemed that Kelly had just wasted away over the course of the weekend.

Later, Kelly's parents packed up Kelly's belongings to take back to their house. 'Not that,' her mother said when her husband reached for the mirror that had fallen to the floor. It must have been too heavy for the hook he'd put up. *It certainly feels heavier,* he thought. 'We'll just take back the things brought from ours.' she said. 'I never did like that. Just get rid of it.'

*****

Julie strode along the road. She reached a little charity shop, and something glinted in the sunshine as she passed, catching her eye. Although she wanted to get home as soon as she could, she felt compelled to stop. There, resting against an old wooden dresser, was a pretty antique mirror, its silver frame shining. A feeling of longing overcame her; she had to have that mirror. *That'll look lovely in my room,* she thought, as she pushed through the flaking blue door and into the dim interior.

'Oh, be careful with this,' huffed the volunteer as she lifted it from the display, 'it's heavier than it looks.' Julie smiled as she paid the woman and clutched her parcel to her.

Help

Lois Maulkin

I was singing as I came around the side of Mrs Barber's house, banging the gate behind me and strolling into her garden.

In those days I was living in an ancient out-building at the back of Mrs Barber's cottage. It was an old saddlery, comprising a miniature kitchen and bedroom, with four small-paned windows which swung open across her roses. Mrs Barber had beautiful roses which seemed to bloom for most of the year.

She was old-school enough to regard her garden as an outward expression of the orderliness of her mind. She was a well-spoken widow in her eighties, slightly prim in a bridge-playing, 'I've survived the Luftwaffe you know,' kind of way but twinkly with it. She was always pleasant.

We got on rather well, Mrs Barber and I, despite my gales of raucous laughter at all hours of the day and night, and my penchant for playing The Beatles far too loud. She'd knock at the door of my little kitchen with a bunch of cut stems from her garden, handing them over and smiling, saying, 'Some flowers for a lady.'

'When I was younger, so much younger than todaaaaaaay,' I was bawling as I rounded the corner of her house. I stopped short, key in hand. There was a man on my roof.

'Hello?' I called up. 'Can I help you?'

'Hello love. I'm fixing your leak.'

I remembered that Mrs Barber had mentioned someone would be coming to do it. She had noticed my Heath Robinson and, to my mind, utterly charming kitchen ceiling arrangement of lengths of green guttering held up by blue gingham ribbons to guide rainwater into the Butler sink, when she'd handed over an armful of snapdragons the previous week.

'Great,' I said, opening my door and stepping inside. 'I expect you'd like a cup of tea?'

I put on a record –The Beatles' *Help* LP – and made two mugs of tea. When I turned to take his out to him I was surprised to find him standing in the kitchen, just behind me.

'Sorry love,' he said, taking the tea, 'didn't mean to make you jump. My name's Dave.'

He was about five feet eight or nine I suppose, greying, not terribly clean looking but, to be fair, he'd obviously been up on the roof for some time so he might well have stepped out of his house that morning looking like he was going to the palace. He didn't now. He looked like a chimp that usually shaved but hadn't bothered over the Spring Bank Holiday.

'This your room?' he asked, going through. I followed him. 'Beatles, eh?' He stood in the middle of the floor, with his feet apart, holding his mug and looking round thoughtfully.

I felt ever so slightly uncomfortable. I'd expected him to stay outside. It wasn't really a big deal. I'd offered him a cup of tea and I couldn't say, 'Please go outside,' without feeling like the least pleasant person on the planet. But everything just felt a tiny bit wrong. Without actually saying 'Wouldn't it be a great idea for you to get back up on the roof where you belong?' I tried to steer his thoughts that way. I said, 'Will it take you much longer, the repair?'

He took a suck of his tea. 'Nah,' he said, 'not long.'

'What, a day or so? A week?'

'Nah. Be done in an hour,' another suck, 'if I don't fall off.'

I heard that downward run of notes that precedes the, 'When I was younger...' and in my mind's eye I saw Dave bouncing off slates and thudding on to the pathway.

'God, do you do that often then, fall off?'

'Nah,' he said. He took another slurp of tea.

'Have you ever broken any bones?' I asked, intrigued despite myself.

'Nah, I know how to fall, see. Parachute training.' He threw back his head and drained his tea and I felt myself relax slightly – he would soon be clambering back up his ladder.

'Useful for you, in your line,' I said, taking another sip.

'Yeah, but the self-defence has been more useful. Everyone should learn it. Specially women. So many dodgy men about these days.'

I found myself nodding vigorously.

'My daughter was attacked on a train last night,' he said, crossing the room to put his mug on the table.

'What happened? Was she okay?' I asked, pleased that he was moving in the direction of the door.

'Yeah, I'd taught her some self-defence moves and she fought him off. You ever learnt any self-defence?'

I shook my head. I heard John, or was it Paul? singing 'I never needed anybody's help in any way'.

'I can show you, if you like.'

To this day I don't know why I said it but I heard myself saying, in a very tiny, polite voice, 'Yes, please.' I think I expected him to produce a business card and tell me to phone for class details or something but within a heartbeat he was standing behind me.

'I'll pretend to be an attacker,' he said, 'I'll do it like it's real, so it feels real,' and he'd got his hand across my shoulder and down the front of my T-shirt and inside my bra and was having a right old rummage about. Bizarrely, I remember quite clearly thinking, *I've given him permission to do this. It would be rude to tell him to stop now,* and standing there hideously shocked that I had been paralysed by my own manners.

It felt as though he was there, groping away, for ages, but it can't have been terribly long, as the line about my independence seeming to vanish in the haze was still playing when he said, 'Now push me off with your elbow.' I obligingly did so and he withdrew his hand, saying, 'And that's all there is to it.'

He left the room then, saying, 'Don't mention this to anyone, they might get the wrong idea, I was only trying to help you, like you said I could,' and I sat on the bed in a bit of a daze and listened to the rest of the LP without actually hearing any of it. I could hear Dave scuttling about on the roof and I felt a bit sick. I thought perhaps the milk had been on the turn.

Two weeks later, I was having tea with Mrs Barber in her garden. Birds were singing and daisies had popped up in the lawn. She poured from a pot, the spring sun splashing down into the cups.

'How's the roof now?' she asked. 'I do hope there aren't any more leaks? Have a Bourbon.'

'It's totally fixed, thank you,' I said, biting my biscuit. I could hear The Beatles, just gently, drifting from my window.

'Interesting man, Dave,' said Mrs Barber, pulling her shawl around her and stirring her tea. Her eyes narrowed just perceptibly as she said, 'He showed me some self-defence moves.'

The hair on my arms sprung up and I felt the back of

my neck prickle. It was horrible to think of Dave assaulting Mrs Barber the way he had me. My mouth hung open and, I'm afraid to say, a bit of biscuit fell out.

'Sorry about that,' I said, retrieving it. 'You mean he came up behind you, attacked you and invited you to nudge him away with your elbow?'

'You too, I take it,' Mrs Barber replied, lifting the teapot to gauge its fullness and looking at me over her half-moon glasses.

'Yes,' I said, thinking. *He must try the same with every woman he does work for. That could be several a week.* 'Should we tell the police?'

'No need,' said Mrs Barber, winking. 'The day after he did your roof he was at Emmeline Saunders, over the common, re-pointing her chimney.'

'Emmeline you play bridge with?' I asked, picturing the tiny, bird like woman with the soft grey bun and powdered face.

'Yes, that's her. He showed her some self-defence moves too.'

'Poor Emmeline. Is she all right?' Nausea stirred.

'Yes, Emmeline's fine. I'd called to warn her he might try it and we were ready for him,' Mrs Barber took a sip of tea.

'We?' I asked, intrigued.

'Yes, I thought I'd pop over. We little old ladies need to stick together. Unfortunately, just as Dave was climbing off his ladder on to the roof Emmeline and I somehow fell against it and it toppled over. Silly of us, wasn't it? A bit unsteady on our feet these days. It turns out Dave wasn't quite as good at falling as he'd thought.'

A smile spread across my face. 'What happened?'

'He fell.' From my window I heard The Beatles singing, 'Down, down, down'.

'Was he hurt?'

'Oh yes,' said Mrs Barber, her face expressionless, pouring more tea, 'really quite badly. It's amazing what they can do with spinal surgery these days but I'm afraid Dave won't be mending any more roofs.'

There was a moment of shocked silence.

'Won't you be arrested?' I asked.

Mrs Barber shook her head. 'Not without Dave's past behaviour being brought into the open. I doubt he'd want that to happen. Anyway, it really was an accident.'

I thought of all the hundreds of women Dave had probably molested over the years. I thought of all those women who would never be able to lose that horrible memory of Dave's hands on them, all the years they would feel stupid to have been tricked into letting him do it, all the years of reliving the shock and despising themselves. And then I thought of all the other women who now would be spared that awful experience.

'I don't think I've ever seen your roses looking better, Mrs Barber,' I said, smiling and taking another biscuit.

The Break

Michele Hawkins

Tilting her head, she felt the warm sun on her upturned face. Her sandals protected her feet from the sharp floor which was reflecting the sun back from millions of tiny pieces of crushed glass and shells. She strode purposefully across the ground, reaching a boulder of grey rock, and sat on top of it gazing out across the azure sea. It was as still as a pond, sunbeams dancing on the surface like tiny fairies, their wings fluttering, playing chase, but sometimes it could be grey and menacing, hostile. Today she felt that she could jump from the clifftop to be embraced by a warm, salty hug but it was too far to do so safely. Over the years she had seen people attempt it only to be dragged down to a watery grave. *No*, she thought with a shiver, *she would not be jumping, however much the sea flirted with her.*

Presently, she was awoken from her reverie by the sound of angry shouting. Glancing around, she saw two women standing opposite each other, mirroring stances with legs planted firmly apart, hands on hips, taking turns to lean into the other's face, expelling a string of expletives that ripped through the hot, hazy air, courteously taking turns to deliver insults. It was really quite amusing although the content of this exchange was definitely not suitable for a warm Sunday afternoon in May. She turned away to resume her meditation and, gradually, the disturbance faded into the background. Taking long slow breaths, she imagined the feel of the sea gently supporting her weight, caressing her while she floated on her back with her eyes closed to the penetrating rays of the sun.

The shrill sound of the bell made her jump. Insistently ringing in loud bursts of five seconds it travelled right through her making her teeth and hands clench. She hated that sound; every day for nearly eight years the bell had invaded her very being, stripping away her dignity and making her feel helpless. Some would say it was what she deserved but she did not agree. They did it on purpose, of course, she knew that. Even so, she wished they would change it to a comforting tolling bell like those in a bell tower but no, they knew its power. Defiantly she sat on her warm, smooth boulder trying to ignore the noise and restore her earlier calm. She counted the rings that signified the end of fresh air and a return to the dank, dark building behind her. She wouldn't go. What could they do?

The clanking of chains behind her answered her question. Four wardens approached with batons drawn in readiness as the tannoy burst into life announcing the misdemeanour of life prisoner 1113 on the island prison of hell, thirty-five miles from the nearest mainland.

SUMMER

Patchwork

Sue Duggans

Pioneering open heart surgery was in its infancy in 1964. That's when Grandpa was cracked open from neck to navel and his life was saved. His scar was visible evidence of this and his active life, some thirty years later, testament to the expertise of those early pioneers.

Grandpa enjoyed nothing more than to sit on a Sunday afternoon with little Teddy on his knee. Teddy was his tenth grandchild but only the second to bear his family name. He was very fond of Teddy and his feelings were reciprocated. Teddy liked to rub his hand over Grandpa's weekend stubble and mess his neat silver hair which amused them both.

It was early June and Teddy's fourth birthday was fast approaching. It was a blisteringly hot Sunday and the family called in to see Grandma and Grandpa who was outside cutting the lawn. Sweat beads drizzled down his face and he'd removed his T-shirt in an attempt to keep cool. Tom and Emily, Teddy's older brother and sister, settled inside to watch TV. Teddy skipped and hopped outside shrieking with delight. Grandpa switched off the lawnmower and spun round with a broad smile. Teddy stopped in his tracks.

Grandpa's a monster! he thought as he saw, for the first time, the patchwork which was Papa's torso. Tom had a picture of a monster stuck to his wardrobe door in the bedroom which the boys shared. He called him Franky Stein and would sometimes kiss his grotesque image, which made Teddy laugh.

Yes, Grandpa is a monster! Grandpa knelt down and held out his arms. Teddy ran towards the house. He flew through the lounge and into the kitchen where Mum, Dad and Grandma were drinking tea. He buried his head in Mummy's lap and sobbed.

'Whatever's wrong?' she asked. Teddy didn't lift his head. Mummy lifted him on to her knee and he held her tightly. Even the offer of a cuddle with Grandma and some of her chocolate cake didn't placate him.

'Maybe he's sickening for something,' Mum said, 'although he was fine at the beach.'

The family cut short their visit and made their way home baffled by Teddy's distress. Once at home, Teddy went straight to his room and sat staring at the image of Franky. This is where Tom found him.

'What's wrong, mate?' his brother asked as he sat beside Teddy and put a reassuring arm round his shoulder.

'Grandpa's a monster. I saw it. He's just like Franky,' Teddy spluttered.

Tom was a bright and intuitive ten year old and, in

an instant, understood. He pulled his little brother on to his lap and sensitively explained in simplified terms the reasons for Grandpa's scar.

Teddy turned to his big brother and smiled. 'So Grandpa's not a monster?' he queried.

'No, mate. Far from it!'

Teddy slipped to the floor and went downstairs, reassured. Tom carefully removed the Frankenstein poster, folded it and popped it away in a drawer.

Father's Day

Barbara Sleap

It had to be Father's Day, the day Alison would take her revenge, revenge for the seven years of misery inflicted on her by her husband, Brian.

This was an important date in Brian's calendar; the day their little girl, Chloe, gave him a homemade card and presents made at her nursery school; the day he insisted on having a big roast dinner with too much wine; the day Alison usually incurred more bruises and degradation. Oh yes, he was a good father and adored Chloe, but the time had come to put an end to the torture before Chloe realised what a monster her daddy was. This year, Brian would get nothing but her revenge.

Brian Chaplin had swept Alison off her feet seven years ago. She had truly loved him but even after six months of marriage the signs were there; a little push, a not so gentle poke or just a sly pinch. He made comments about what she wore, what she cooked and who she saw. The house was never clean enough, never tidy enough, however hard she tried. Alison had naively thought that things would change after the birth of little Chloe, now aged four, but if anything, the incidents became more secretive, more intense. The pinches became punches, the pokes became bruises or cuts and the pushes made her fall over.

Alison had confided in no one, too ashamed to admit that her marriage had been a mistake. Instead, she had become an expert in disguising cuts and bruises with make-up and the right clothes. Brian told her she was frumpy, but she couldn't wear anything sleeveless, short skirts, or tops with a low neck. She kept her hair long which helped to cover the telltale marks on her face, and she wore trousers and maxi skirts along with long-sleeved blouses.

Of course, no one would believe her, everyone loved Brian, Brian the joker, the Brian who helped people out, oh yes, he put on an Oscar-winning performance of being a perfect husband and father. But no one knew the real Brian, the cruel Brian, the mean, violent Brian.

So, after months of scrupulous preparations made on her secret mobile phone and the computers at the library, she was finally ready, her arrangements and phone calls culminated on this day in June, Father's Day.

Brian had worked his night shift and arrived home as usual at 6.30am looking grumpy and tired. He glowered as Alison handed him his tea in the must-have blue Spurs mug, his toast lightly browned, real butter and spread with Hartley's seedless raspberry jam. He sat at the table and unsuspectingly drank the tea, which was heavily laced with finely crushed sleeping tablets, and munched on the toast which also had a sprinkling mixed in with the jam. Alison had to make sure. The tablets were Brian's own, prescribed to help him sleep during the day while on night shift, and she watched as he took two from the packet which he swallowed with the last of the tea. Well, he would sleep today that was for sure. He would probably sleep tomorrow too, well, at least until the milk, sugar and cereal ran out; she'd put some in them as well. Alison had certainly made certain.

He lumbered towards the door.

'See you later then. What time are you picking Chloe up from Mum's? You haven't forgotten what day it is, have you?'

'Lunchtime,' Alison mumbled, 'and no, I haven't.'

With that, Brian disappeared upstairs to bed. Alison waited an hour and crept up to their bedroom. She looked sadly at the pile of Brian's discarded clothes, his shoes and socks strewn where he had removed them. He could do his own washing now; perhaps he'd make a better job of it than she did. She watched his breathing; he was out for the count.

Alison went into the spare room and pulled out two packed rucksacks from the wardrobe, one for herself and one for Chloe. They would only have the basics for a while but she would buy things at her first destination, a quiet woodland holiday site outside York, two nights in a two-bedroomed caravan that she had actually booked for a week. She had her train tickets and also their passports, not that she needed them for her final destination in Inverness, but one day she might.

Alison had found a lovely refuge for abused women and their children in a remote village. It was a gorgeous country house that promised safety and peace. From now on her name would be Leonie Fellows and Chloe would be Carrie; she would get used to it, children get used to things easily. An appointment had been made at a York hair salon she'd found online, where her long mousey locks would become short and blonde. Chloe's lovely curls would have to go too.

She had secured herself enough money to last for a few months, some from her father's inheritance, which Brian thought was invested and she had slowly removed over the last year. Some she had squirreled away from the wages she received from her part-time job at the local Tesco store. She had handed in her notice a month ago and had worked until Friday, so she had her P45 and a month's holiday pay too.

Alison looked around the kitchen. She used to love this house but now she hated it and what it stood for. She shut the front door and, without a backward glance, headed for her new life.

*****

Brian woke slowly and looked at the clock. It was 6.00pm, he had a thumping headache, his mouth was parched, in fact he felt as if he had a hangover. He was generally up by three. Where were Chloe and Ali? Normally Chloe would rush in and jump all over him. He tried to call out but he seemed to have lost his voice. God, he needed a shower and a cup of tea.

Where was that bitch? She knew it was Father's Day, his special day. Chloe should be here with his card and present, excitedly waiting for him to open them. There was no smell of roast beef either, no sound of voices downstairs as Chloe watched her favourite film *Frozen*, for the umpteenth time. Surely they couldn't be still at Mum's? Alison never wanted to stay there long.

He rolled out of bed, he felt terrible, was he ill? He grabbed his dressing gown and tripped over his shoes. The bitch hadn't even tidied up his clothes. He really needed a hot drink, a nice milky coffee or something.

He staggered down the stairs, gripping the banisters as he descended. The house was silent. He would have to phone his mum, but first he needed a drink, hot and milky with plenty of sugar. That would do the trick.

Marrying Paul McCartney

Kim Kimber

I can smell oranges. Someone nearby is peeling them. I can visualise the skin being slowly ripped from the flesh, juice running down their fingers.

It is a warm day. I don't know how I can tell but the sun is shining. My feet and legs are bare and the long grass tickles my toes. I am not alone; someone is with me, laughing; a man, I think. Yes, he is taller than me and good-looking, with long lashes and a lopsided smile. The oranges are being chopped on a board and they smell so good as they are popped into a jug with ice. The man hands me a glass of amber liquid. I take a sip. The drink is bitter-sweet and cool, Pimm's; my favourite.

The man leans over to remove a stray strand of hair from my eyes and I can smell the tang of orange on his fingertips. He whispers in my ear, 'Don't leave me.'

I am fighting now; something is dragging me away from the scene, from the sunshine and the lovely man. I struggle to hold on but the image fades and the darkness threatens to pull me under.

But something else catches my attention; a sound,

music, someone is singing. I recognise the voice, the tune but I can't recall from where. An image pops into my head; a dance floor, I am swirling round and round. I feel dizzy, spun around by a man, he is laughing. People are watching us but I don't care. I am happy. It's the same man with the oranges and I feel safe for an instant but then he starts to fade. I reach out for him, try to call his name, but he is gone.

His name! If only I could remember it maybe he will come back and this time he will stay. It is lonely here on my own. I listen carefully as the song is replayed. It is not a modern tune, I realise. The music is rhythmic, and reminds me of an Oompah band, nothing like the songs my children listen to. The thought hits me like a bullet. My children! I have children; the idea surprises me. Where are they? Are they safe? Who is looking after them? Panic starts to rise as the darkness reaches out to me. I try to fight but it is too seductive and, this time, I succumb to the blackness.

*****

There it is; that song again. It is playing over and over. I am surprised to find myself humming along to the lyrics in my mind. The tune sounds old-fashioned but somehow I know that it is very important. Who is singing? Is he the man from my dreams? He has a lovely voice; soothing. A name comes into my head, 'Paul'.

Could that be the man with the oranges? 'Paul', it is a good name, simple, strong.

I am swirling again, round the floor in my white dress. I am happy as I dance to the music with Paul. He smiles down at me and I recognise him from my earlier dream. We continue spinning around until I am dizzy and the edges of the image start to become blurred. I am losing him again. A voice echoes round my head, 'Hold on, stay with me.'

The images flash on and off, like someone repeatedly flicking a light switch. I am confused and disorientated. Through it all, I am aware of someone sitting by my side, holding my hand; Paul. He seems to be key helping me to escape from my prison. The song is playing again but now it panics me rather than soothes me, as if I'm not supposed to be here. Why can't I remember? The tune won't stop. It is being played over and over, on repeat. I want to scream but there is no sound, only this suffocating darkness; oranges, dancing, Paul.

Paul McCartney! It comes to me in a rush and I am pleased with myself for remembering. The song is 'When I'm Sixty-Four'. It is about love and staying together forever. That's it. We are at a wedding; our wedding. I am Mrs Paul McCartney. This breakthrough, though a relief, exhausts me and I drift away just as Paul is asking me if I will still love him when he is old. I try to imagine the orange man's face, lined and wrinkled with age, and smile as he sings me to sleep.

'Sixty-four'! The number is familiar. Is that the number of my house? I try to remember but find that I can't picture where I live. Am I at home now? It doesn't feel homely, this prison, and it is dark, so dark. I wish that someone would open the curtains and let in some light. Maybe it's my age? No, it can't be. Sixty-four sounds old and I don't feel old. I am that young girl swirling around the dance floor with the man who smells of oranges.

Maybe, if I concentrate really hard, I will be able to piece together the jigsaw that is my fragmented mind. How did everything become so muddled? I can remember walking to the shops, in sunshine. It was a warm day, I can feel the sun on my skin and the smell of oranges. No! I am getting confused. That is another memory.

It is raining, really hard, and I don't have a coat. It is a freak storm. Thunder booms around me. Lightning hits nearby and for a moment, everything is lit up. The crash is so loud, it stuns me and I don't see the car. Then I woke up here, in darkness.

This is not a prison. It's a hospital. I realise this as I open my eyes and see the man sitting by my bed. He is the same man from my dreams but with salt and pepper hair and a worried expression that emphasises the lines in his face. 'When I'm Sixty-four' is still playing in the background. The song was played at our wedding and we danced to it. But I did not marry Paul McCartney. My husband is called John and he has been sitting by my bed, every day since the accident, waiting for me to come round. A crate of oranges rests by his side that he is slowly working his way through. Peeling them one at a time, hoping to spark a memory and bring me out of my coma.

Bev's Special Jam

Pat Sibbons

I look at the row of freshly sterilised jars, all lined up and ready to receive the latest batch of jam. It's cooling in the preserving pan and will soon be ready to decant into the jars. Today I have made raspberry; the fruit has been grown in my garden and I know it will be delicious.

Forty minutes later and the jam is in the labelled jars. My special jar with its slightly different label stands apart from the others, with the lid off. There are a few rules that I always apply to my jam-making enterprise:

1. A high standard of hygiene is to be maintained at all times. Utensils are scrupulously cleaned, jars are properly sterilised and cats kept out of the kitchen.

2. The best quality ingredients are always used. There are never any manky old berries in my jams.

3. The special jar is always labelled with the special label and kept separate from the rest of the jars.

4. The jam is prepared just before it is to be sold.

My next outing with the jam is tomorrow. I have a stall booked at a church fayre in Westbroom, a village ten miles away. Part of my weekly routine is to check local papers and the internet to find out when and where I can find outlets for my produce. Again, there are rules as to how I go about this:

1. The stall is booked to sell handmade cards. Some fayres and fetes insist on seeing a food hygiene certificate, which I don't possess.

2. I never give my real name or address – for the purpose of this exercise I am Anne Reynolds.

3. I only sell my wares away from my local area. I think it is safer this way.

4. The special jar was to be kept away from the rest of the jam at all times. I don't want any accidents.

The phone is ringing. I walk jauntily up the hall. I am always in a good mood before a jam outing.

'278412.'

'Hi Bev, it's only me seeing how you are.'

It's my cousin Sadie. She lives in the next village with her husband, Simon. She only moved there recently and I haven't even been to the new house yet. She usually rings a couple of times a week for a chat. Both she and I are the only children of sisters. She married and now has two lovely children, both at university. I did not. Her mother lives, mine died. We have always been close and I see her more as a sister than a cousin. She includes me in all her family occasions and I love them dearly.

'I'm fine thanks. Not up to anything special. I have been in the garden this morning having a bit of a clear up.'

Sadie doesn't know about my jam enterprise. She knows I make jam, she can see the preserving pan when she visits, but she doesn't know about the fetes and table sales. I think that is for the best.

After a good old chinwag with Sadie, I return to my work. The final ingredient is ready to be added to the special jar. I take great care with this, adding the right amount. Just enough. Mission completed and everything packed away, I take a nice mug of tea into the lounge.

Sitting in my armchair, my eyes meander around the room, bringing back memories. The large, worn armchair opposite is Mother's. Her favourite cushion remains untouched. The little table next to it is still home to her nail file, little red clock and medication. Just as she left it. I look at the mantelpiece and the photo of us. Christmas 2010. We had such a lovely day and Mother looks so happy.

I miss her so much. I sip my tea and have a word with myself. There is, after all, no going back to the past. Spit-spot. On we go.

I arrive at the village hall in time, but not too early. Too early is bad. It draws attention to you and I am all about blending in. The hall is bustling. Knitted baby clothes, landscape paintings and homemade cakes everywhere. I am allotted a table next to a wildlife charity. Good. Nothing too jazzy to compete with.

I get out my cards. I have always enjoyed crafts and the making of greetings cards has long been a hobby of mine. Having spread my white tablecloth over the table I arrange my cards; Birthday, Sympathy, New Baby, New Home…then I place my sign 'Anne's Handmade Cards – Beautiful cards for all occasions'. This part of the display complete I get out my jam. Only a few jars with a beautiful written sign, 'Homemade Jam'. If someone with a clipboard comes around and queries jam being sold on a card stall I will look dismayed, offer apologies and put it away. So far this hasn't happened. To be honest, everyone here is only interested in making money; for the church, for the Guides, for the charity, and for their own pocket.

The footfall is busy from the start. Women pushing buggies, gangs of little Brownies; all life is here. My cards are going well and I have sold a jar of normal jam. No one in my target market has shown an interest in my jam and therefore my special jam remains unsold. I know exactly, when I see them, who deserves a jar of my special jam:

1. She must be elderly, but spritely.

2. She must be smartly dressed but not too showy.

3. She must be pleasant but not a sweet old lady.

4. She must live alone. I don't want her sharing the special jam.

In fact, she must be just the kind of old lady Mother would be now if she hadn't died. Mother and I were 'The Two Musketeers'. It had always been just us. I didn't know my father. He left when I was a baby so Mother and I were very close. She was an intelligent, sharp-witted woman. She held herself very straight and dressed impeccably. I nursed her through her long illness. She became immobile, incontinent and her eyesight deteriorated. She refused to be dressed in anything other than nightgowns. The doctors had failed to diagnose her condition until it was too late to do anything much about it.

One afternoon, Mother was sitting in her chair, opposite mine, watching the lunchtime news. Although her eyesight was now poor, she watched an item that featured an elderly lady. She was being interviewed at her front door about crime in her area. She was clearly quite old but stood steady on her legs, spoke clearly and strongly and was neatly dressed. Mother said, 'That is the kind of old lady I wanted to be.' A tear rolled down her cheek. I was heartbroken.

A lady has stopped to look at my wares. She is turning over a 'Good Luck' card. She is clearly older than she looks. The hands are a giveaway. She is dressed nicely and holds herself well.

'It's a lovely day,' I say trying to make conversation.

'Yes, but there is a nip in the air.'

I think she may be the one. She looks over at the jam.

'I make it myself,' I say. 'Home grown fruit. I bet your husband would love a nice bit of raspberry jam on a scone this afternoon?'

The woman looks interested.

'I'm on my own now but I'll take a jar and this card.'

Perfect. I take the card and the jar, turn my back on her to put it in a bag and swap the ordinary jar for the special one.

'I hope you enjoy it.'

'Thank you,' she says.

*****

The phone is ringing.

'278412.'

'Bev? It's Simon. I'm sorry Bev but I have some terrible news. Sadie died in the night. I just couldn't wake her this morning. The ambulance people think it might have been a heart attack.'

I can feel my knees beginning to buckle and am

grateful that there is a chair next to the phone table.

The funeral takes place two weeks later at the church in her village. The flowers are so beautiful and the church is packed. Sadie had many friends. There is that sense of injustice hanging in the air when someone dies before their time.

I am sitting in the front row, next to Simon and the children. We await the arrival of the coffin. I turn and look at the congregation gathered behind us and my eye rests upon a familiar face. I rack my brain trying to remember where I have seen it before – and then I remember. It is the woman who bought my last jar of special jam. What is she doing here? The craft fayre was ten miles away!

'Simon, who is that?'

'Oh, that's Edna, our next-door neighbour.'

I shift uncomfortably on the hard, wooden bench.

'Oh. I thought I had seen her somewhere else, maybe in a village miles away?'

'You might have,' he says. 'She has a daughter in Westbroom.'

I begin to feel sick. 'She is really lovely,' continues Simon, 'only recently she gave Sadie some jam she had made herself. I can't stand raspberry jam myself, but Sadie loved it.'

Water Music

Lois Maulkin

So, after he'd done that thing where he went down the river on a baby grand for charity, Barry, cold, wet, exhausted and sunburned, went home for tea.

'How did it go, love?' shouted Wendy from the kitchen. Her voice rode into the hall on rolling waves of scent from the Bolognese pan.

'Well, I'm still alive,' said Barry, peeling off his wet running shoes and socks. 'Bit of support from you might have been nice, though.'

'I know. Sorry love, I couldn't leave Mother on her own again. Not today. Not with her phantom pregnancy and everything. Go well, though, did it? Did you go the distance?'

Barry told her about his afternoon bobbing downstream on the beyond-hope Bechstein. About the eddies, the chords, the leaking, the swirling, the sliding, the tipping, the sinking, the spluttering and the grateful, gasping reaching of the bank.

'Did you finish your sandwiches?' she asked, setting the table for the three of them.

The Bolognese was good. Warm and savoury and

everyone felt much better once it had been eaten. Wendy's mother gave a small burp and tittered, wiping her chin with a paper napkin. 'Ooooh, it's a hungry one, this one,' she said, look down at her belly and smiling serenely.

Wendy rolled her eyes. 'Mother, you're seventy-seven,' she said. 'You don't leave the house and you don't actually know any men. Don't you think it's a bit unlikely that you're pregnant?'

Wendy's mother blushed and said, 'Well, unlikely it may be, but it's happened.' She asked Barry if he'd look out the cot from the loft for her in the week to come.

'Imminent then, is it?' he tutted. 'Who's the father?'

'I'm not entirely sure,' said Wendy's mother. 'May be the Archangel Gabriel. Or perhaps the milkman.'

'We don't have a milkman,' said Barry getting up from the table.

Wendy flicked him a glance that said 'leave it'. He took a step backwards, holding up his hands in surrender and went out to his shed for a private can of beer and *The Archers*. He set up a deckchair in front of the lawnmower, switched on the radio and sat back, eyes closed. Barwick Green, the smell of creosote, and fatigue washed over him. He closed his eyes. For a short moment he reflected on how like a cat he was – asleep with his ears awake. And then he was back on the shiny black back of the piano, bobbing and twirling downstream, reeds and willows and lilies gliding by, and soft grey water working below him, taking him away from where he had come from, away from home, away from himself. In his dream, he took a seat at the piano, and played as it swirled on down to the estuary, his fingers darting like fish across the keys.

He woke suddenly, as Wendy's panicked voice shot into the shed. 'Barry! Mother's gone!'

His initial reaction was a sudden and enormous lifting of the spirit, but that was quickly dispelled as inappropriate and he dragged a look of concern on to his face.

'You mean she's...she's dead?' he said, coming out of the shed and trying not to sound too hopeful.

'I don't know,' said Wendy. 'I don't know where she is. One minute she's taking the newspaper and a carton of milk up to her room, the next she's vanished.' Panic cracked her voice and introduced a thin wobble of humourless laughter.

They searched the house. Barry even went up into the loft in case she'd gone up after the cot. Not there. They went round the block. They went up and down the High Road.

'She'll be looking for the father,' said Wendy suddenly, so they hurried to the church and the milk depot. Not in either of those.

The evening sun spun long shadows out across the grass as they searched the park, Wendy weeping openly and Barry cursing under his breath.

'We need to call the police now,' said Barry eventually. Wendy nodded and pulled out her mobile phone. 'Shall we just check at home again first?' she asked.

As they reached their doorstep, screams could be heard coming from inside.

'Oh my God,' said Wendy fumbling with her key in the lock and, after what seemed like several years, letting them both in.

As they shoved the front door open and scrambled indoors, a horrible, high-pitched yowling sound filled their ears and they ran up the stairs.

There was Wendy's mother, squatting on the bathroom floor. 'It's coming!' she yelled, her twisted, mottled, arthriticky fingers pulling up her skirt. 'My waters have broken!'

'Jesus wept!' said Barry.

'Get a doctor,' said Wendy, splashing across the bathmat towards her mother.

'Get a doctor? But she's not really having a baby, is she?' Barry often took refuge in what seemed to him to be salient facts.

'She needs a doctor because she is not well,' Wendy hissed venomously. 'Oh God, this is milk all over the floor.'

Barry stood up and exhaled vastly. 'I can't do this any more,' he said, walking down the stairs.

Wendy was calling. 'Barry! Barry! Come back!' as

he reached the front door but he walked unhurriedly to the pavement, got into his car and drove through the half-light to the water's edge.

He could see the baby grand under the waves, sitting solidly in the middle of the river with reeds swaying around it as though appreciating music only they could hear.

Is That What You Meant Do?

Michele Hawkins

'Is that what you meant to do?' Jenny shouted from the back door.

Lisa slowly turned round, her eyes glassy, unseeing and bloodshot. Jenny shuddered as she took in Lisa's appearance, trying not to look at the bloodstained knife in her left hand. Lisa stood still for what seemed like an eternity before whispering, 'No, I wanted to kill him.'

*****

Jenny and Lisa had been friends for several years, meeting, as often happens, at the school gates when their eldest children started at the local primary school. Gradually their lives became more entwined as their husbands met and liked each other.

Over the years, they shared many memories and had been going to the same caravan park on the Jurassic coast in Dorset for two weeks every summer. It was always a noisy, happy, relaxed and alcoholic time. They were normally lucky with the weather and nothing was better than being on the beach with the kids, Jenny's three boys and Lisa's two, digging to try and reach Australia, or burying their dads up to their necks in the sand.

Only, the last holiday had felt different to Lisa. She couldn't put her finger on it but she had an uneasy feeling that had refused to diminish. She had spoken to Marcus, her husband, about it but he had dismissed it as nonsense. Maybe she was working too hard; her publishing job was quite demanding, and she hadn't been sleeping very well, but she was unable to totally shake the feeling that all was not quite right.

Lisa still couldn't say when she knew, but it had sort of crept up on her, like layers of an onion being peeled away one by one. Looking back, it was all so obvious; the furtive glances, the brushing of hands slightly too lingering, the work meetings that overran. When her eyes were fully opened, she considered her options. Leave Marcus, but what about her two beautiful boys who both adored their father? Kick Marcus out? But that would have the same effect on her boys. After agonising for several days, she decided to pretend all was okay.

Well, this hadn't worked for long as the next evening Jenny sat at her table, eating the food she had slogged over, drinking the wine she had carefully chosen, all the while making eyes at her husband! Pleading a headache, Lisa went up to bed where she re-evaluated her situation. She decided that she would have it out with Jenny, an option she realised she hadn't considered before. Lisa loved Jenny like the sister she had never had and even now she wanted to somehow come out of this, still friends.

The following day she invited Jenny round for a coffee when hesitantly and tearfully she told her everything she had witnessed and the conclusion she had reached. At first, Jenny tried to deny the affair but very soon was sobbing, begging for Lisa's forgiveness. She said she didn't know why she was doing it but that excitement and risk in an otherwise predictable life was addictive. Jenny agreed to end the affair and Lisa totally believed her.

Over the next few months, Lisa began to relax her guard. Indeed, Marcus was more attentive, not in a guilty way, just how he had been before, buying her flowers occasionally and noticing when she had made a special effort with her appearance. Neither made any mention of the affair, which would be odd to many people but it seemed to suit both Lisa and Marcus. The annual holiday was on the horizon and Lisa was looking forward to it.

*****

The boys were staying with Marcus's parents for a few days as it was the summer holidays and this gave Lisa time to pack for Dorset without constant interruptions and arguments about what to take.

She was in her bedroom sorting out the final

101

washing load when she noticed what looked like mud on one of Marcus's work suits. Pulling it from the back of the wardrobe, tutting to herself as she would now have to add dry cleaners to her long to-do list, she started to empty the pockets. Something small and hard was in the jacket breast pocket. Withdrawing a mobile phone that she had never seen before, she sat down heavily on the bed. Holding her breath, she flicked open the cover and switched it on. Only one name appeared on the contacts list, Jamie. Feeling puzzled, she realised that she had been half expecting Jenny's name to appear. How absurd! She mentally shook herself. Curious rather than anxious, she turned her attention to the text messages.

What she saw made her blood run cold. Text after text declaring undying love and planning the best way to tell Lisa and Tom, Jenny's husband, while on holiday, that they needed to be together and had decided to set up home, in Dorset! The worst part for Lisa was not the shock of the betrayal by her best friend and husband but that her boys' lives would now be ripped apart.

Lisa had felt a powerful surge through her body like an electric shock. With her heart hammering and blood pounding in her ears, she had practically flown downstairs and into the kitchen where she swiftly took a knife from the butcher's block. Walking across the room to where Marcus was sitting with his back to her eating his breakfast, she had plunged the knife into his back screaming, 'Bastard!'

*****

Lisa sunk to the floor, curling into a ball on her side. The knife slipped from her grasp and lay next to her, glistening in the sunlight streaming through the kitchen window.

Cautiously, Jenny crept across the room to the body slumped forward over the large farmhouse table, normally a place for socialising noisily over rustic fare accompanied by copious amounts of wine.

He was sitting in a chair, breakfast laid out in front of him. A low moan escaped from his white lips. Jenny moved closer so she could hear what he was trying to say but as she did she suddenly felt a great force on the back of her knees. Crashing to the ground, she had no time to put out her arms and so took the full impact of the fall on her shoulder.

Winded and in considerable pain, she lay still for a moment but before she could fully comprehend what had happened, Lisa was standing astride her with the knife poised, still dripping blood, 'And now I'm going to kill you, too.'

The Woman On The Cliff

Kim Kimber

It is windy and exposed up here and I sway slightly in time with the breeze, bottle in hand.

I can see a family on the beach below. The man is chasing two small boys across the sand, their identical blond heads bobbing rhythmically as they dart around in excitement. Their laughter drifts up to me and I take a long swig of cheap, vinegary wine.

The boys evade capture and veer off towards the wide expanse of sea and splash into the water, doggy paddling away from the shore. The man dives in and quickly reaches them with strong, powerful strokes. I am too far away to see, but I know that his body is taut, lean and muscular. They bob about together for a while and then start jumping in and out of the wind-whipped white horses, shrieking as the swirling water sucks them under and spits them out.

Another woman watches from the beach. She stands and takes a few steps towards them, camera in hand, ready to preserve the moment; a happy snap of a day out at the seaside. She clicks away for a few minutes and then returns to the picnic blanket, stretching out lazily with a book.

Long-limbed and slim, with dark hair piled up on her head in a bun, she wears the kind of strappy red bikini not designed to get wet. Her casual body confidence tells me that she is used to people observing her, a woman more attuned to turning heads on the sun-saturated beaches of the Med, than disrobing on the breezy English coast. I take another slug from the bottle and the sour taste burns the back of my throat.

A short while later, the swimmers return to shore and the woman jumps up to greet them with towels and, so I imagine, indulgent smiles. The boys are quickly wrapped and mummified as they chatter away noisily. The staccato soundtrack to the scene drifts up to me like a poor radio connection… 'You should see…fish…this big…dived in…waves…huge…hahaha…tickles.'

I move closer to the edge of the cliff, greedy for more, but the height and the heat makes me dizzy. I should step back but I am transfixed by the little group, unable to move. I watch as the man takes out a knife and begins to attack what, from up here, looks like a large, green ball – a watermelon. He expertly hacks into the fruit and hands out chunks to the boys, the perfect antidote to the saltiness of the sea. The boys flop down on the blanket, each leaning against one of the adults as they devour the juicy flesh, and I visualise twenty lively toes wiggling happily in the sand.

I recall other times in this same secluded spot, when

I too had basked in the sun and danced in the waves. Our special place. The memories keep coming, one after the other, the clarity for once not lost by the deadening effects of the alcohol; bodies entwined, the salty taste of his skin, his hand on my belly waiting for the twins to kick.

The boys are up now, restless, picking up plastic spades and buckets, pulling at their father. The three of them begin to dig furiously and the beginnings of a castle quickly take shape. It will be a huge creation, I am sure, with turrets and a moat, masculinity measured by the yard. The children run backwards and forwards to the sea and fill buckets with water to cement the results of their labour. Their movements are practised, familiar.

The film in my head continues to replay other occasions. Dark days and nights when the thick blanket of depression smothered the joy of motherhood. The solace of drink, blotting out the constant cries and demands. Then the arguments, fights and shame.

The wine is warm and unappealing but I take another mouthful, blurring the edges of the day. Seagulls cruise overhead and I wonder what it would feel like to fly, to swoop down to the group below and snatch up those boys, one in each claw, dipping my wings in farewell, mocking their father with my victory cry.

The four of them are on their knees digging, creating a strong and secure fortress to keep out unwelcome visitors. The castle will hold its position for a long while before eventually being washed away by the incoming tide until there is no trace. Little by little, it will be eroded until there is nothing left – just like the dying moments of our love.

But I am a mother still. I remember the last time I saw our sons as they left with their father. 'It's just for a short while,' he said, as he bundled them away to a new 'safe' life. 'Once you get help the court will allow you to see them.' The judge decided differently and denied access, condemning me as unstable, unfit and unworthy.

There may have been a way back for me, to try to get to know my children again, but their dad sought a different kind of comfort. Now all I can do is watch as the woman on the beach builds a life with my family. The bottle is almost empty and I drain the contents quickly and toss it aside in disgust.

The gulls caw and cry their warning, as I lean unsteadily into the wind. One of the boys looks up. I can't tell which as, even close to, they are identical. Jack and Julian; my sons.

The child points and waves. The group stop building and Luke, my husband, leaps up and starts shouting in my direction but his words are drowned by the cawing of the gulls. I wave to the twins and try to turn back but the ground beneath me begins to crumble. Then, I am spinning and turning in the air, weightless, flying back to my boys.

A Letter To My Younger Self

Josephine Gibson

Oh Kathleen.

You were silly to trust that boy. Silly and naïve.

But maybe Ma and Da were silly too. They were too trusting, taken in by his soft Irish ways. He'd turn up at the gate and Da would love the craic. You'd stand there in your short-sleeved cardigan and your best shoes, handbag over your arm, waiting in the shadows while they gossiped and laughed, until Da said, 'Away – be gone with you. Bring her back safe and sound.'

He didn't know then how those soft Irish ways, those soft Irish eyes, could seduce a silly young girl like you. He thought that boy was marriage material and he'd got another daughter off his hands. Well, he had, hadn't he? Not in the way he thought though.

You were silly to trust those nuns too. Silly old biddies, telling you what was best. What did they know? They'd never held a soft-downed, newborn daughter in their arms, never felt her nuzzle in for a suckle, never felt what it was like to touch the one person in the world who loved you when your family had cast you out.

'Don't be too fond of her,' they said, that time they

caught you crying in the nursery. 'Think of her future. She's better off in a good Catholic family with her own mammy and daddy.'

The day they took her away, you should have snatched her and run and run. You could have done something but you just stood there and felt ashamed and let them do it. And took your little suitcase and boarded the boat and came to Liverpool and never looked back. Or so you thought.

And you were silly, silly, silly, never to say anything. To pretend you were a sweet, young Irish virgin and fool the first man that came along who earned a wage and could keep you. To lie, to pretend that narrow bed in the boarding house was your first time, when your heart ached for laying in that fresh meadow of home, your lover pressed hot down on you, his warm breath on your neck as you surrendered yourself to him.

And you kept pretending, but you could never trust anyone again. Not even your own children. You could never let them come as close as your first one and they knew there was a piece of your heart they'd never have.

And you were silly, supremely silly, when that letter came. Too scared to let people know the hussy you are, afraid of the gossip, of the twitching window nets. So you wrote back and said no, no contact, even though your heart was breaking to hold her in your arms again.

Well, Kathleen, she wouldn't want to know a silly old woman like you anyway.

Memories Of Summer

Michele Hawkins

Annie gazed wistfully out of the window. She saw sky as blue as the Mediterranean Sea, with the odd fluffy cloud sailing by, glistening silver in the morning sun. Annie tried to remember the last time she had seen such a beautiful morning, the birds chirping with glee and the breeze coming in through the open window, gently brushing her face.

However, all she could recall was the torrential rain of the last week or so, relentlessly drumming against her window and leaving lakes on the grass outside that could easily play host to a few ducks before gradually draining away, leaving muddy puddles. She had heard old Mr Tom whistling through his teeth, clearly disgusted by the destruction of his manicured lawn. He was always out there in any weather tending the garden. Nothing dared to disobey him; everything preened and pruned to within an inch of its life. Mind you, the garden really was rather lovely, even in the depths of winter when the bare trees reached out their bony arms to the grey sky, imploring the sun to show its face, however weakly. The regimented line of trees drew the eye down the garden towards the summerhouse, painted a soft sage green. Yes, Annie could forgive old Tom his rather terse manner; he was not a sociable man, obviously preferring his own world, but he was a wizard when it came to creating a garden for all seasons, especially in summer when the smells and colours evoked memories of foreign lands.

When Annie was a young girl, her father had taken her and her mother on foreign adventures to faraway exotic places. Places that were an assault on the senses, the pretty pastel coloured houses, the heavy scent of frangipani hanging in the air, the shouting in foreign tongue of the brown-eyed, bare-footed children busy making mischief and their parents scolding them; the taste of new foods – pungent garlic and burningly hot chilli peppers.

The beach had always been Annie's favourite place to visit. She had enjoyed the feeling of the sun, and the hot sand between her toes, the palm trees swishing in the warm breeze and the occasional plop as another gave up its fruit. After basking in the sunshine she would run as fast as she could down to the sea, whooping with pleasure as she plunged her hot, sore feet into the soothing water. Then she would wade in further and further until she disappeared in the salty spray. Swimming with long, slow strokes, she luxuriated in the feeling of calm, listening to the waves stroking the shoreline.

Occasionally, she would fully immerse herself so that the sounds of the beach disappeared and all that she could hear was the sound of her heart, the beat getting louder as her lungs began to strain until she was forced to burst through the surface, gasping for air. As her heartbeat settled and her vision cleared, she would gradually become reacquainted with the sights and sounds of humanity around her.

Remembering the past was all that Annie could do now. Her future held nothing but death; her present, endless hours of listening to the noises of the nursing home where she lay bedridden, unable to move or speak and, now, even the pleasure of eating had been stripped from her.

Becoming aware of the breeze from the open window gaining strength, she willed a carer to come into her room and pull the blanket up to her chin, but feared they would probably close the window while bustling around speaking to Annie as if she was a child, a deaf child at that. They had given up expecting a response long ago and so filled the silence with inanity until finally they buzzed off to annoy another inmate

Anyway, it wouldn't be long now; she had heard the doctor say that her body was slowly shutting down. Like switching off a computer, her life was fading into blackness. She smiled as she closed her eyes, inviting the silence to embrace her.

AUTUMN

First Day Nerves

Sue Duggans

Clothes laid out in readiness.
Restless sleep,
Alarm clock beep.

Cereals at breakfast bar.
Big day starts,
Racing hearts!

'Now it's time to brush your teeth.'
Smile is bright,
Hiding fright.

Shoes are polished, bag is packed.
Out the door,
Trembling jaw.

First day tensions mounting fast.
Early start,
Heavy heart.

Walking quietly, side by side.
Mum and boy,
Fear, not joy.

Up the hill towards the school.
Boy and mum,
Heartbeats drum.

Children enter by the gate.
Take off coat,
Lump in throat.

Tender kisses, heartfelt hug.
Straighten tie,
Tear in eye.

Teacher gently takes a hand.
Anxious frown,
Tears roll down.

'Don't cry, Mrs Klein,
Harry will be fine.'

Davey

Barbara Sleap

It was Friday and Davey was on his way home from school, the end of his first week of walking home on his own. Well, he was eight and a half now and he wasn't a sissy.

He was so intent on his packet of wine gums and thinking about the trip to the park to collect conkers later, that he didn't immediately notice a tall lady walking alongside him. She had yellowy hair which was pushed back by big black sunglasses and had those shoes with 'spinnetto' heels that went 'tip tap' on the pavement.

'Hello, Davey.'

Davey wondered how this lady knew his name. His mum and dad had always warned him not to talk to strangers, so he put a red sweet in his mouth and carried on walking with his head down.

'Are wine gums your favourites, Davey?'

He looked up at the stranger. She looked like someone but he wasn't sure who.

'Mmm,' he muttered, 'but I like Smarties best, especially the orange ones, they're really orangey.'

Davey continued walking but the lady put her hand on his shoulder. Davey didn't like that very much and walked faster.

'I've got some Smarties in my car, Davey, it's parked just over there.' The woman pointed towards some parked cars further up the long, straight road that led towards Hillside Gardens.

'My little dog is waiting for me, he's called Jock.'

Davey's head jerked up and he stopped momentarily.

'My dog's called Jock, too.'

'Well, that's a coincidence isn't it? Do you want to come and see him, and I can give you those Smarties.'

The lady's hand pressed harder on his shoulder. The thought of Smarties and a puppy called Jock was tempting but Davey said, 'No, thank you, I have to get home 'cos my mum is waiting, we're going to take Jock to the park and collect conkers. She promised because I got a gold star for my dinosaur story yesterday.'

'Your mum won't mind, Davey. I'm a friend of your dad's and–'

Before she could finish, Davey realised who she was. It was the lady his dad used to be married to, he had shown him a photo but in it she had brown hair. His dad said she had hurt him once and had been away for a long while, and if Davey ever saw her he must tell him.

'–he said you could come with me any time.'

Davey was walking really fast now and he wished

the lady would go away, he wanted to see if he could jump three paving stones in one go, he did two yesterday and he was sure he could jump three. Besides she was hurting his shoulder. 'Tip tap, tip tap' went the red shoes.

She stopped suddenly at a silver car and roughly pulled Davey to a halt. His school bag fell off his other shoulder and he hoped his lunchbox had stayed shut, his mum had been cross when he dropped his bag once and yogurt had slopped on to his maths book.

Davey could hear a dog yapping inside the car. Still holding on to him the lady opened the passenger door. Davey could see the black and white puppy on the back seat, jumping up and down at the window excitedly.

'Come on Davey, get in, the Smarties are in there.' She pointed to the glove box under the dashboard but she didn't let go of him.

Davey stood still – the lady looked cross now. He didn't want to get in the car, he needed the toilet. She was really hurting his arm as she tried to push him on to the seat. He knew what he must do. He twirled round, lifted his right leg and gave her a hook kick just like Lee Yong had shown him at Monday's Karate lesson. Davey already had his orange belt and was training for purple now.

The woman immediately let go of his arm but tried to grab him with her other hand so Davey gave her his best upper rising block which made her stagger. He followed this through with a hikite punch to her right side and she fell to her knees giving Davey the chance to run.

He ran and ran, without looking back, until he reached his gate. Mum and Jock would be waiting to go to the park and he wanted enough conkers to burn on the bonfire on firework night – they crackled and sort of exploded; it was really exciting.

Even if he was called a sissy, Davey thought he would probably ask his mum to meet him after school the following week.

Time And Tide

Pat Sibbons

I picked my way carefully across the line of seaweed and assorted rubbish that had been deposited by the storm the previous night. It reminded me, oddly, of the costume I had worn as a drama student, performing in street theatre, one hot summer. I had played the Water Witch, bedecked in green and blue strips of rags, as close as poor students could get to a costume representing waves and seaweed. It had been such a laugh. Carefree, sunny days before full-on adulthood took hold. Life hadn't panned out as I had expected. But then, whose ever did?

Now, at the water's edge, I stopped, enjoying the wind blowing against my cheeks. I had always loved this place. Mark had loved it too. The cove was secluded, difficult to reach easily and therefore we were usually the only people here. It felt safe.

*****

'Hi, I'm Mark. Good to meet you. I hope you will really enjoy working here.'

The man standing in front of me had one of the nicest smiles I had ever come across. Warm. Open. I watched him walk down the open-plan office. The woman I was with told me Mark was one of the senior partners and he was heading the project that I would be working on. For the next few weeks I met every day with him and the small group he had put together for the project. He was an attractive man, but not so attractive that he was arrogant. He made me laugh often and I looked forward to getting up and going to work each morning.

After not making it as an actress, I had carried resentment around with me like a heavy bag of shopping for years. I hated every job I'd had as it wasn't what I really wanted to do. But now I was actually enjoying work, thanks mainly to Mark. He seemed to really listen to everything I had to say. No idea that I put forward was dismissed out of hand.

On my third week, there was a leaving do on the Friday night. It was being held in a local wine bar that I had never been to before. I made my way there after work, not really looking forward to it as I still felt like the new girl. I didn't want to admit it to myself but secretly I hoped Mark would be there. It seemed everyone from the office was there when I arrived, except Mark.

The leaver bought me a large glass of chilled white wine and I chatted with a couple of people working with me on the project. It was quite pleasant but I wasn't really enjoying myself. I realised this was because Mark wasn't there. I bought a round of drinks and was preparing to leave when I felt a light tap on my shoulder.

'You're not going already are you?' Mark stood in front of me, beaming. He bought some drinks and we stood talking to the others for some time. People began to drift away; some back home to their families and others to continue the night with a curry. Mark and I stayed in our seats, tucked away in the corner of the wine bar.

We talked for hours about everything. We had so many similar interests. Mark listened as I told him about my dream since childhood of acting. He seemed to really understand my lack of fulfilment as I hadn't achieved it. He told me about his family. He had been married for twenty-four years to a girl he had met as a teenager. They had two grown-up children and life had been good for many years.

But he and his wife had grown apart. She suffered from depression and Mark worried about her. The children had left home and she had her own interests. They even took separate holidays. As Mark spoke he looked deep into my eyes and I could feel his sincerity. The eyes are supposed to be a window to the soul and I could see that this man had a good soul.

The time flew by and then it was midnight and the wine bar was closing. As we stood outside waiting for cabs, he told me how much he had enjoyed the evening and that he would like to meet up again soon. He leant down and kissed me very gently on the lips.

That night my mind just spun. I knew my developing feelings were, on paper, wrong. But to me, they felt right. On Monday morning I was hesitant entering the office. How would Mark react to me? Would he regret Friday night? I needn't have worried. Mark was his usual self. Just before lunch he came over to my desk.

'Do you fancy a sandwich at the pub?'

Of course, I said yes, as I wanted to be with him. I just felt so at ease with him. Lunchtime flew by and as we were about to leave I asked him if he would like to come round to my flat later in the week for dinner. He looked at me very earnestly and said, 'I would really like that but are you sure?'

We both knew what he meant. This would change everything. Everything did change. The next five years were the happiest of my life. I found another job soon after our relationship began, to avoid anyone finding out about us. We were always careful not to be seen by anyone we knew. I refused to see our relationship as an affair. Affairs are tawdry.

Despite the compromises that had to be made because of Mark's situation, we managed. I accepted Christmases without him, not being invited to his son's wedding, and so many other events. The time we spent together was all about us. As often as we could, we drove to the cove. He would take the day off or manage to get away over the weekend. We would lay out the picnic blanket and stay there for hours. Just us.

Each month or so, Mark would bring me a gift. He never said it, but we both knew the situation wasn't ideal and I think the gifts were his way of trying to make things better for me. He knew I loved hearts and he usually bought me these. All sorts; stone, ceramic and one I particularly treasured, a crystal one. Gifts of love.

He promised me that things would change. When the time was right, and his wife was strong enough to accept it, he would leave her and we would set up home together. One day.

*****

The first I knew that something was wrong was when Mark didn't arrive at the flat for dinner one Monday night. He had been at a family christening on Sunday and so I hadn't seen him at the weekend. He didn't respond to my texts and phone calls and eventually I went to bed and lay there worrying. This wasn't at all like him.

The next day I tried again and eventually, at lunchtime, I rang his office. I was put through to his secretary. I lied and said I was a potential client who had spoken to Mark recently. She said she was sorry, but Mark had been killed in a car accident and was there anyone else who could help me? I put the phone down. Of course no one could help me. No one could do anything. That was that. No happy ending. I wasn't even entitled to grieve. I couldn't attend his funeral. He wasn't mine after all. I never intended to hurt anyone and wasn't going to start now. In my mind, as they never knew, they were never hurt. Mark's family sounded great and I didn't want the memory of their father to be anything but a good one.

No one sent me sympathy cards, no one popped round to see how I was. I had never told anyone about Mark. My friends and family knew I was seeing someone but they thought it was just a very casual relationship – nothing serious. I just said we had both agreed to go our separate ways. I wasn't entitled to be broken-hearted.

The sound of circling gulls brings me back to now, standing here alone on the beach, as in life. I am done with crying. I pull from my bag the small trowel and from my pocket the crystal heart. I dig a small hole and perform my own ceremony. My own funeral. My own solitary goodbye to the love of my life. I kiss the heart and place it in the hole on our beach. Carefully I level the top. Brushing the sand from my knees, I take one last look at the final resting place of my heart. 'Goodbye Mark.'

Bring Me The Head...

Lois Maulkin

'Is that what you meant to do?'

'What, you mean reverse the car across next door's lawn and destroy their fountain?' My knuckles were white on the steering wheel. 'Yes, darling,' I spat, 'of course that's what I meant to do.'

With gritted teeth I ground the gears and shot forwards, across an array of mixed heathers and on to the street.

In the rear view mirror, I could see his lip was quivering.

I took a deep breath and said, 'Mummy's sorry darling. I'm not cross with you. I'm cross with myself.'

He was sounding a bit gaspy and I knew tears were coming, 'So why did you be mean to me?'

No. I couldn't have it. I couldn't have his tears and snot and howling all over the car, there wasn't room for it all. Not with it as full as it was with my guilt.

'Don't cry, my precious,' I said, valiantly. I felt momentarily proud of how I was holding things together, managing a note of sanity. I remember thinking *sometimes, all unknown, we make such superhuman effort every day* and then inside me, at just about the point between my ears where my neck meets my skull, something went ping, or bang, or snap...or...well anyway, it just went.

I pressed my foot on the accelerator and my eyes closed and my mouth opened and there was a roar as the car hurtled thirty feet into the back of a skip.

We were not hurt. We spent the afternoon in the Accident and Emergency department, anxious and bored and doing the same twenty-four piece jigsaw over and over again. Then, when it was dark and cold, we were let out, waited for a bus in the drizzle and came home to our empty house.

Telly on, heating on, kettle on. 'You're turning everything on,' he said, looking up with big eyes.

'I am, aren't I?' I said, slotting bread into the toaster.

There was a knock at the door. I opened it and my neighbour came in, with a stone head in one hand and an exasperated look on his face.

'Simon, you won't believe how truly, terribly sorry I am,' I said, getting out mugs and teabags.

'My alpine heather bed is like a scale model of the Somme.'

'I'm so very, very sorry, Simon. It was an accident. Is Marie very angry?'

'Obviously,' he said. 'And your car's a write-off, too.'

He looked at me thoughtfully and said, 'You are

okay, aren't you? I don't want to be rude, so forgive me, but you haven't seemed yourself. Marie and I were talking about it the other day. We wondered if you might be, well, perhaps struggling? To cope? I mean, it can't be easy, all on your own.'

I felt tears well up and turned away, busy with the kettle, so he wouldn't see my mouth stretch out unattractively the way it does when I cry. It's not pretty when I cry, I don't mind telling you. My bottom lip goes purple. A tiny sob squeaked out. He crossed the kitchen and put an arm round me, awkward.

I turned and pressed hesitantly into his warmth and breathed in the beautiful scent of him. Like those old white roses that smell of toffee on summer afternoons, clean hot water and the fresh sharpness of crushed tomato leaves, bruised coriander. I sucked in a huge, soothing, joyous lungful of him, and felt a kind of peace trickle through me, starting across my shoulders and seeping down my back, across my hips, down my thighs.

And almost no guilt, just a tiny bad smile, hidden in the shoulder of his jumper.

It had, obviously, been what I'd meant to do.

Meeting At Fireworks

Josephine Gibson

Saturday, 5th November dawned unseasonably warm and Sarah shook her head as she strode down the seafront on her morning walk. *It must be a sign of global warming,* she thought, *I'm sure it used to be colder when I was a child.* Or perhaps that's a mistake of memory – had she merely remembered one cold autumn night that cancelled out all the other, milder experiences? Yet somehow it seemed wrong to enjoy warm weather at this time of year. It clashed with her childhood memories of the contrast between raging bonfires and frosty breaths and made her wonder what the world was coming to.

She had found it difficult to care about anything over the past few years. Nothing had seemed very important after Peter had died. Making changes for the future seemed pointless when your life existed in the past. Yes, she had made an effort, put on a face, gone through the motions; but in reality the emptiness inside her *was* her. It had engulfed feeling, purpose, and compassion for others. She had become her grief.

As ever, she looked for the boat with the red hull. She'd met an acquaintance of Peter's, once, and he'd mentioned he kept a boat moored in the water near their home. It had become a talisman for her, a sign that she was still connected with Peter, and there it was, pointing down the estuary. Peter, not a sailor himself, had always speculated whether this meant the tide was going in or out and she couldn't remember now what he'd concluded. The familiar sharp pain tugged at her, she'd never be able to ask him now.

She stood, facing out to sea, the mild wind catching strands of her hair, caressing her and reminding her she still existed. This was her routine, her ritual, her memorial of Peter, performed at the beginning of every weekend, so that no matter what had been arranged to distract and soothe her, she could fiercely assert that she would not forget, could not be comforted and could therefore keep him alive just a little bit longer.

And yet her strength of feeling was fading and she was frightened by the change. Her grief had, in its way, been a purpose in itself and without it she didn't know who she was or what her future held. She realised it meant she was beginning to think again and to recognise she had time ahead of her. Empty time that needed to be filled. *Perhaps*, she thought, as she turned for home, *she really ought to do more for the environment.*

Instead, later in the day after she'd been imprisoned by the rain, she felt stir crazy and decided that watching explosions launching who knows what noxious substance into the atmosphere was definitely preferable to watching a worthy documentary on television.

As she stumbled out of the house, zipping her raincoat hood up under her chin, she reflected that a year ago she would have welcomed wet weather and an excuse to do nothing. She would have gained a wry satisfaction that the clouds matched her mood. She felt ashamed that she would, in fact, have been pleased that other people's Bonfire Night was ruined. It had seemed right that other people should suffer. Why should she be alone in her suffering? Now, however, she recognised that the pent-up energy she felt after being indoors was a positive force – yet it angered her, because the further she moved forward in her life, the further she left Peter behind.

Probably it would have been better if she'd arranged to attend the fireworks display with friends. She felt as though she was the only person on her own as she joined the groups of pedestrians walking towards the beach. She squared her shoulders and breathed out: this was something she would have to get used to. There were families everywhere; dads carrying their children on their shoulders, mums wrapped in see-through plastic capes grimly holding small hands, and grandparents swinging children between them. She smiled as she saw some children playing with sparkling wands and then, 'whoosh' a luminous bead launched up into the air above her and a small boy scrabbled at her feet to catch it as it descended.

'Mind the lady, Reece,' a man called, and Sarah turned to smile and say she was OK, but they had already been swallowed up by the crowd.

She began to feel claustrophobic amongst the masses of people with a single purpose and so she broke free and walked briskly away. As the sounds behind her began to fade and she felt the uneven grass of the common beneath her feet, she made herself stop, she had to be brave. She had to stop running. She turned. She could watch the fireworks from here and then slip quietly home.

'Hello, it's Sarah, isn't it?' a voice said and she looked round to see a middle-aged man in a puffa jacket with a wellington-booted boy hitched against his hip. He had his back towards the light and she didn't recognise him.

'Sorry, it's a bit gloomy, you probably can't see me – I'm Ray, I was at school with Peter.'

'Oh,' she tried to think of something to say, or remember where she might have met him. Probably at the funeral.

'How are you getting on? I was so sorry to hear about Peter and sad to miss the funeral. He was such a decent guy, great sportsman when we were at school. Wish I'd kept up with him a bit more after A-Levels – but you know how it is, everyone off to university, then I worked abroad–'

'Grandad!'

'But I remember I bumped into you both one year, New Year's Eve party–'

'Grandad!'

'It was round at the – at the – oh, some couple I can't remember their names now–'

'Grandad! Wee wee,' the little boy shouted.

'Whoops! Sorry, we're off to find the nearest bush! Stay there,' he commanded and strode away purposefully, depositing the child on to his feet, pulling the boy's trousers down and allowing him to joyfully arch his back and release a curve of urine that puddled into the sandy soil. Pulling the child's pants back up, he guided him back towards Sarah with a gentle push behind the shoulders.

'This is Jonny – my grandson – lovely little devil – I know, I know, I look far too young. Product,' he winked at Sarah, 'of my misspent youth.'

'Oh, right,' she said, unsure of how she should answer, 'Peter and I–'

'You've got a son, right? Grown up?'

'At university.'

'Best place. Keep him busy. Bright like his dad?'

'Well, yes, we're – I'm – very proud of him, how he's coped, it hasn't been easy–'

'I should think not. Look,' the little boy was tugging at his hand, 'I've got to get back to the family. I'm here with my daughter and son-in-law. Are you on your own? Come and join us.'

'Well, I–' she meant to refuse, embarrassed, but at that moment the swish and boom of the first rocket made her jump, she hadn't expected it.

'Come on, Grandad! It's starting!' Jonny shrieked and ran forward. Ray caught him by his anorak hood, turned, caught Sarah's hand and tugged her to join them. Laughing, she realised she had met a force of nature and it suddenly seemed more important to move forward than to resist.

Fire Escape

Trisha Todd

It's tough living outdoors. A new housing development has fenced off a large part of my patch, places to hide are a lot more difficult to find and food is scarce.

This night, I crept along the hedge, head down, not wanting anyone to see me – I knew to my cost that it could be dangerous on the streets if you are on your own. I've been kicked before, and several times a car has nearly driven over me! I don't usually go out until it's good and dark, but tonight I was hungry and chanced to come out early to see what I could find.

The hedge was decorated with spider webs, the diamond droplets catching the dying rays of a watery sun. The last autumn leaves were banked up under the branches; a jewel-box of gold, bronze, yellow and red overlaying each other, rustling as I passed. A breeze caught them and I stopped to watch nature's ballet as they swirled over and around me. It was getting colder and I wondered if the snow would come early this year.

Another noise intruded and I shrank back against the branches as the gang approached. I'd seen these boys before but, this time, they had a large, chocolate-coloured dog with them, its great pink tongue lolling out of a mouth set with sharp teeth. It was off its leash and heading my way. I froze – perhaps if I was still enough it would not notice me, but I was unlucky; head down, it made its snuffling way directly to my hiding place.

'Wotcha got there, Bozo?' the lad in a blue jacket shouted as he made his way towards me. The Labrador was distracted and I took my chance to push through the hedge into the neighbouring field and ran as fast as I could. I heard the boys kicking up the leaves and laughing. 'There's nothing here, you daft dog,' one of them shouted. 'Come on, let's take him home, it's getting too dark to see him.' I could still hear their voices as they carried on down the road and thought I'd better find another hiding space in case they returned.

Across the piece of scrubland, I could see a pile of branches, caught with old newspapers and various pieces of rubbish. I'm not too fussy where I lay my head, and the wood and paper would keep the worst of the wind out, so I made my way over. A large branch arched above some smaller twigs, the space underneath just large enough for me. I shuffled in carefully, pulling yesterday's news over me as I went, and drifted off to sleep.

It was fully dark when I woke with a start. A loud bang sounded nearby, followed by another, then a flash of light. I could hear voices, lots of voices. I edged forward and stuck my head out from my hiding place.

Crowds of people were standing a few yards away, including the gang I'd seen earlier. I looked around – was that dog with them? A drift of mist curled in front of me, obscuring my view, so I shuffled to the side for a clearer look.

'Wow, look at that go!' someone squealed. Light flared again, together with a crackling sound, and the shadows danced. The mist had a funny smell and, as it got thicker, my eyes began to water. I moved again but nudged the branch, which fell, cutting off my retreat and exposing my hiding place.

'Hang on!' shouted a familiar voice. The boy from earlier was running in my direction, his blue jacket now in his hands. Before I could move, he had swooped towards me. Lifting me high against him, he covered me with his coat and turned to head back to his friends. They looked from me to my shelter, the straw-stuffed Guy perched on top smiling as the flames licked at his bonfire seat.

The lad pointed into the dark. 'Poor little hedgehog. It'll be safer over there,' he said, carrying me towards the copse in the distance, as another firework lit up the sky.

Remember, Remember

Barbara Sleap

Rose walked around the house checking that things were in place for the annual family firework party. Relatives would soon be arriving, excited children and their parents wrapped up warm, each carrying colourful boxes of fireworks. The youngsters would struggle through the front door with homemade images of Guy Fawkes stuffed with newspaper and dressed in old unwanted clothes, the heads made of brown paper bags painted with ghoulish faces and topped with various forms of headwear; school caps, knitted hats or ragged straw sunhats.

Rose smiled in anticipation; her own two sons, Danny and Rob, were getting dressed noisily upstairs and her husband, Sam, was already attending to the bonfire heaped high in an isolated corner of the garden. She could see him from the window, breaking up an old bedside cabinet ready for cremation. Yes, it would be a grand fire tonight.

Rose entered the warm kitchen, just as the doorbell chimed. Danny and Rob hurtled down the stairs, both wanting to be the one to let the first guests in and get the party started. She checked the sausages, chicken drumsticks and burgers, all laid neatly on trays like soldiers on parade, ready for the oven. The jacket potatoes were sizzling on the lower shelf and several tins of baked beans filled a large pan on the hob. From then on there was a constant flow of family members, both old and young, keen to enjoy the evening feast and fireworks. The night sky was fast becoming alight with rockets showering their sparkling contents to the 'Oohs' and 'Aahs' of the children.

The fire was lit to loud whoops and cheers. Sam, Jimmy and Fred started the display; they were the only ones allowed near the pile of fireworks laying in a large crate well away from the fire and the guests, in line with the much advertised 'Firework Code'.

Giggling children, their faces aglow with pleasure, were given hand-held sparklers and began to write silly names as the sticks sizzled and spat. Rose watched as the men carefully lit the tapers of 'Golden Rain', 'Roman Candles' and 'Crackling Fountain'. Later, there would be rockets soaring in all directions, launched from the line of milk bottles placed strategically on the grass. 'Catherine Wheels' would spin on the fence posts, noisy bangers and 'Jumping Jacks' would explode, scaring the children as they leapt around the terrace.

Rose felt happy; it was all going so well. She peeped around the door of the sitting room where old Aunt Lena and Uncle Harry were watching the events from the warmth of the blazing fire in the grate, he with his glass of whisky and smoking a pipe, she with her knitting and a glass of sherry. Rose smiled at them fondly and slid from the room.

At last, the display was almost finished and Rose was back in her kitchen where Grace and Winnie were piling plates with steaming food while Bonnie poured hot chocolate into a variety of waiting mismatched mugs and cups. With their plates loaded, everyone dispersed to warm up by the fires in the sitting and dining rooms. Rose listened to the chattering and laughing as her family ate their food heartily and she felt a moment of nostalgia as she remembered other family gatherings that had taken place in her house.

It was getting late, and the children were looking tired. Time to go, but not before Sam filled glasses with brandy and looked round at his family.

'Thanks for coming everyone. This has been a sad year.' He faltered as he raised his glass for the toast. 'The first Bonfire Night without our Rose. We all missed her but I'm sure she is with us in spirit.' Glasses chinked and tears were shed as the toast rang out, 'To Rose.'

They didn't feel Rose as she twirled around the room touching each and every one of them.

Large Print

Pat Sibbons

Doreen parked her shopping trolley in the corner next to the front desk. This was all part of her Thursday morning routine. A trip to the market to collect her fruit and veg. A mooch amongst the stalls for bargains. A chat with some of the stallholders and then on to the library.

The library assistant greeted her with a warm smile. 'Morning, Doreen. Did you enjoy these?' she asked, taking the books from Doreen and scanning them.

'Not bad, not bad. Got anything new in?'

'Yes, a few historical and romances and some crime you may be interested in.'

'Ooh, lovely,' said Doreen. She may have looked like a sweet little old lady but she loved nothing more than a gritty crime novel. The higher the body count the better. The more grisly the violence, the more she enjoyed them.

Doreen made her way over to the large print section. An elderly man was sitting at the table. He looked up from his book as she approached.

'Good morning,' he said.

He was very smartly dressed in a collar and tie with neatly combed hair. Dapper, that was the word.

'Morning. Bit chilly out there today.'

Doreen scanned the shelves containing the crime novels to find the tasty new ones she would enjoy devouring later. Her eyes came to rest on one she hadn't read; *Their Last Hope*. That sounded like her kind of thing. Doreen took it from the shelf and placed it on the table where the man sat. She turned again to the shelves to find another book to join the first.

'Do you enjoy crime novels?' The man looked at her quizzically.

'Yes. Bit of escapism never hurt anyone.'

'They're not for me I'm afraid,' said the man. 'I prefer historical fiction myself.'

Stuffy old fool, thought Doreen. She found another book she hadn't read and hurriedly picked it and the first up and turned to leave.

'Goodbye,' said the man. Doreen ignored him.

On the following Thursday, Doreen parked her shopping trolley as usual, returned her books and made her way to the large print section. The man was there again. He looked up as she approached, smiling broadly.

'We'll have to stop meeting like this,' he said.

Good Lord, thought Doreen. 'Morning,' she said. She turned towards the shelves quickly to avoid eye contact with him.

'You took off a bit quickly last week. I hope it

wasn't something I said?'

'No, no. Each to their own. If you prefer reading about dusty old castles and kings with gout, good for you. I prefer something a little more exciting.'

The man looked crestfallen.

'Oh, it's just that I was a policeman and so I like my escapism a little bit more gentle. I saw such terrible things I really don't want reminding.'

'I see.'

'I'm George, by the way.' The man held out his hand.

'Doreen,' she said as she shook the hand. Doreen turned back towards the shelf feeling guilty for judging the man so harshly. She found another couple of crime novels she hadn't read and pulled them down.

As she made to leave, George smiled at her and said, 'I hope you enjoy your books.'

'Thank you. I'm sure I will.' Doreen found herself smiling back at him.

Thursday came around again very quickly. Doreen parked her potatoes and carrots in the usual spot, checked in her books and headed towards the large print section. No one was there. Doreen found herself feeling rather disappointed. No George. He was very smart and had good manners; qualities that were in short supply today. She had looked forward to having a bit of a chat.

As she checked out her new books, she asked the librarian, 'That bloke George been in this morning?'

'No, he hasn't been in all week. He usually comes in most days for a read. I hope he is all right. I think he lives on his own.'

Doreen collected her trolley and made her way home, hoping that George was okay. She knew how it felt to be alone.

As she headed to the library the following week, Doreen found herself hoping George would be there. Once inside, she turned towards the large print section and her spirits lifted as she saw him sitting in his usual spot.

'Good morning, Doreen. How are you this fine day?'

'I'm all right, thanks. Have you been ill?'

'Yes, a touch of bronchitis kept me at home last week. I'm fine now. I have to be so careful with my chest now that I'm older.'

'Me too. I seem to be laid low for ages if I catch something.' They both smiled at their shared medical problems.

'Did you enjoy your books?'

'Yes. They were both really good. One of them was a real whodunnit. I was amazed at who the murderer turned out to be.'

'That seldom happens in real life. It's usually the first suspect who is guilty and a lot of detective work is quite mundane. I did work on a couple of really major cases over the years though.'

'That must have been exciting. My Alan worked as a

caretaker. I think it was boredom that killed him in the end. Well, I'd best be off. I might see you next week. I need to get home. I live in the block opposite the Co-op and we're having our windows done. I'm the only one on the ground floor so they are starting mine first. Goodbye George.'

'Goodbye Doreen.'

The following Monday Doreen opened her front door to find a carrier bag on the mat. Inside was a hardback book titled *A Policeman's Lot*. She opened the front cover and saw George from the library, a few years younger, staring back at her.

Chief Inspector George Mason, one of the most respected senior officers in the Metropolitan Police. For over thirty years he and his team solved some of the most disturbing crimes the city has ever seen. Rapists, murderers and child abusers have all been locked away thanks to his detective work.

Doreen made herself a cup of tea and settled down to read.

'Morning George,' she said, approaching the table.

'Hello Doreen. Read any good books lately?'

Doreen smiled. 'Yes, I've just finished a really interesting one.'

George returned her smile. 'Would you like to join

me for a cuppa? The café over the road does a really nice lemon drizzle cake.'

'That would be lovely. I'll just pick my books. I thought I might try something different for a change. Something by Jean Plaidy maybe.'

George smiled.

WINTER

Letter To Santa

Barbara Sleap

Dear Santa

I wrote to you last Christmas when I was eight. So, now I'm nine and some of the girls in my class told me there is no such thing as Father Christmas.

Well, I hope this isn't true. It can't be because last time I got all the presents I asked for; a netball goal, a real leather netball, a Pineapple track suit and, best of all, a baby sister. So, I really think there must be a Santa. I've given this letter to my nan to send. If you reply, I will send you my wish list.

Love from Amy

Dear Amy

Thank you for your letter. Well, I've just pinched myself and it hurt so I guess I must be real after all. Please don't stop believing in me because Christmas is such a magical time and magic can be as real as you want it to be. So yes, please let me know what you would like me to organise for you. I have the best job in the world, making children happy in the smallest of ways. It's not just about presents and lots of sweets but being with the people you love and thinking about the real Christmas story. I will wait for your letter and hope that all your wishes will come true.

Love from Santa

Dear Santa

I was really glad to get your reply. Thank goodness you are real because I have some big wishes this year.

I wish my mum and dad would like each other again. They shout a lot, Mum cries and Dad storms out, to the pub I think, because he smells horrible when he comes back. Sometimes they don't talk for days.

My little sister, Emily, is not well, Santa. Mum told me that she won't grow up the same as me, you know, learning stuff, playing netball and singing songs to Little Mix CDs. She doesn't do what she should be doing, Mum says she should be crawling and trying to talk like my cousin Harry, who is a little terror.

My friends won't come to my house any more and say it's because Emily is freaky. I don't think she's freaky, Santa, I think she's cute. She can't help it if she doesn't look quite like me, can she? I know she makes funny noises and dribbles a lot but she has lovely blue eyes and a really cute lopsided smile.

Santa, I don't need any toys or games this year; what I would really like is a puppy. I would look after it cos Mum said she's got enough to do looking after Emily, and Dad doesn't say anything about anything any more. Emily loves puppies. I know she does cos when we're out with her special pushchair and she sees one, she waves her arms about and makes gurgling noises as if she's going to talk. I would love to have a puppy to play with and cuddle, cos Mum and Dad don't seem to do cuddles like they used to and I miss that, especially at bedtime. Maybe if I had a puppy, my friends would come round again and, instead of going to the pub, Dad could take it for a long walk. It might cheer us all up.

Love from Amy

Dear Amy

Your letter makes me think that your mum and dad don't know how you're feeling right now. Perhaps you should all talk and hug each other more. Have a little chat with them at bedtime tonight and tell them what you told me about your friends and how unhappy you are. I'm sure if they knew, they would be upset and try to understand.

I will try my best to help though. I have some special sparkly dust that I will wave over you all on Christmas Eve and I promise you'll have a happy Christmas Day together.

Do you know what I think, Amy? I reckon that little Emily might get stronger as she gets a bit older and you might even be able to try and teach her some simple things, so keep on playing and singing with her. Just because she's different doesn't mean she can't ever learn anything. I'm sure your friends don't mean to say things to you, I think they don't know how to treat Emily, that's all.

As for that puppy, well, you'll just have to wait and see, but I know there is a little black one waiting for a good home!

Love from Santa at the North Pole

Shut-eye

Pat Sibbons

The woman turned her head wearily to look at the digital image on the wall: 02.41 – 25 December 2065.

Another night battling with sleep. She just wished sleep would win more often. Another day with a thumping headache because of tiredness.

She did all the stuff you were meant to do to relax – warm milk, warm bath, cool room but her mind was always churning. The more she tried to push the thoughts away, the more they came. The more she imagined herself listening to waves breaking on a tropical beach, the more rubbish, like the names of the kids in her class at school, forced their way in.

Morning broke and, as she was still awake, she got up and turned on the information system. The usual early morning things were on: 'Do you need help with a difficult relationship? The Blue Project is here to help…'

She wandered into the kitchen where her coffee was waiting for her. She couldn't imagine how it used to be. When people had to wait for things. The advent of cerebral programming had revolutionised people's lives.

Even her coffee machine knew when she needed coffee and how she wanted it. The digital display in the bedroom worked on iris recognition. It only appeared when you looked at it and it knew what information you wanted. Date, time, weather. Endless possibilities.

She sipped her coffee and watched the information display.

'Trouble sleeping? We have what you need.'

They had her interest.

'Sweet Slumbers bring you a revolutionary new pillow, just for you. Contact us on cerebral link 20045 today for a free trial.'

A new pillow. No drugs or implants? It sounded worth investigating. Once she had showered and dressed she contacted Sweet Slumbers. It pleased her to think that, in the past, she would have had to wait days. Since Christmas had ceased to be recognised, the date was not a problem.

The following day the pillow was delivered by a man dressed in the official Service Provider Uniform.

'Good evening. I have your new Restful Night Pillow for you to try out.'

He followed her into the sitting area.

'We will let you try the pillow for a few days. If you find it beneficial and wish to keep it, it costs 2000 bit points.'

'Wow, 2000. That's a lot.'

'I think you will find it is worth every point. Let me

explain how it works. The cause of most sleeplessness is excessive thinking or thinking about the wrong things. The pillow is linked to your cerebral implant and absorbs, for want of a better word, those unnecessary thoughts, leaving you with only those thoughts that won't keep you awake. How does that sound?'

It sounded amazing.

'Is it safe? I'm not going to end up a vegetable in the morning?' she said laughing.

He reassured her that it was totally safe and she duly planted her digital print on the form provided. 'Okay. I just need to link you to the pillow and then you are good to go – to sleep that is.' He sounded pleased with his little joke.

Two minutes later, the man had gone leaving her with a very ordinary looking pillow.

She slipped under the cover and placed her head carefully on the pillow. It felt comfortable enough.

The woman opened her eyes. The clock showed 07.30. She couldn't believe it. She had slept for ten hours and felt wonderful. As she walked to the kitchen, she remembered the dream she had had. She couldn't remember the last time she had dreamt. She had been in a room, alone. The room was empty except for a chair. She had walked to it and sat down. There were no doors or windows. Just white walls. She remembered feeling uneasy but didn't know why and dismissed the dream as she drank her coffee. She had had the best night's sleep for months.

She worked all day and was tired when she returned home. As she ate her meal she was looking forward to going to bed. She so hoped she would have another long sleep.

Wow, she thought when she woke up, 07.30. *Two nights in a row*. This was fantastic. She almost bounced to the kitchen to prepare breakfast. But, as she stood in the shower, the dream began to swim into her mind. She was in the white room again. All had seemed exactly as before, but as she sat looking at the wall it seemed to split to form an opening. A huge rat with yellow eyes had appeared and looked at her. The smell of sewers filled her nostrils as the rat ran into the room and circled her chair. It ran faster and inched closer to her with every revolution. She could feel terror running through her...she hated rats. She had opened her mouth to scream but no sound emerged. She couldn't remember any more. She felt wonderful, full of energy this morning but was now disturbed by the dream. She chided herself. Don't be ridiculous. A silly dream versus being able to function in the morning – no contest!

As she settled down to sleep that night, she turned the pillow over. She knew it was stupid, but wondered if the dreams were anything to do with it. Did it have a good side? Of course it didn't. She lay her head on it and almost immediately sank into a deep sleep.

Again, she was in the room. The uneasy feeling was

filling her chest once more. She could feel it growing into full-blown fear. This time there was a door. Slowly, silently it began to open. Then it was thrown fully open and it slammed loudly against the wall. There was nothing there. She felt herself relax and breathe again.

What was that noise? In the distance she could hear something coming, getting closer, the noise growing louder. The tightness in her chest was immense. The panic inside her expanded with every second. Then it was there, in the door watching – watching her. The thing in front of her wasn't human. It couldn't have been. It seemed to pulsate. As it did she would catch a glimpse of something human within it. It smelt of putrification. It smelt of evil. She saw within the mass a screaming mouth, a severed leg, a clawed hand. She thought the sheer terror of what was before her was going to stop her heart beating. She shut her eyes to escape the horror in front of her.

She opened her eyes. Morning. Her bed. She slowly dragged herself to the kitchen. The nightmare fresh in her mind. She had to speak to Sweet Slumbers. The dreams/nightmares had begun when she had started using the pillow. She connected with cerebral link 20045.

'Well this is highly unusual. I haven't heard of any other clients experiencing anything like this while using the pillow. Are you in good health? Are you taking any prescribed or non-prescribed drugs?'

She assured him that she wasn't.

'But you are experiencing a good sleep level each night? Rested and refreshed in the morning?'

Again she assured him she was.

'Perhaps give the pillow another go tonight. Hopefully, the dreams will have abated as your mind becomes used to your new sleep pattern. If you have another bad dream we can refund your bit points.'

She decided to take the advice given. After all, she looked so much better. The bags and dark circles under her eyes were already disappearing and she hadn't felt this good in years. She was just filled with dread at the prospect of going to sleep tonight.

That night she went to bed later. She took a bath and drank half a bottle of red wine before settling down between clean sheets. She waited for sleep to take her. It was different this time. She was in her own home, standing in the hall. She looked at herself in the mirror. She couldn't see her reflection.

The doorbell rang. Slowly she made her way to the front door. She reached out her hand to open the door but it began to open on its own. On the doorstep stood her mother, as she had looked when she had been about her age. She looked so beautiful. She smiled at her and she smiled back. Her mother held out her hand for her to take.

07.30 – but no digital display on the wall this morning. There is no one to look at the digital display.

164

The woman lies silent in her bed. Peaceful. She looks like she is having the most wonderful sleep. The post-mortem will reveal that she had an undiagnosed brain tumour. It had been slowly killing her for some time. The sleeplessness and headaches had been a symptom. The pillow had just ramped things up in her brain. The disclaimer she signed is very clear. Sweet Slumbers are not liable. Their services will continue to provide help to insomniacs everywhere.

Angel

Trisha Todd

The bitter wind blew down the High Street and into the darkened alley behind the shops. It's a well-known spot for rough sleepers as the police rarely go there, and Jean would often take old blankets that she bought from charity shops, or some of her homemade soup, to give to those poor souls.

That afternoon, as she stirred the broth in the cast-iron stockpot she'd had for years, she had glanced at the photo hanging on the wall of her husband in military uniform, so handsome. With a wistful sigh, she shook her head sadly and concentrated on her cooking. She often felt quite lonely but liked to think she was helping others less fortunate than herself and it gave her someone to talk to. *No one should have to live like that*, she thought, *I'm just sorry I can't do more.*

Ever since her Herbie passed over ('God rest his soul,' she would mutter, after mentioning his name), she lived on her own in their small, two-bedroom flat, just round the corner from the High Street, but she thought it a palace compared to this place. While the shops were decorated with tinsel and pretty lights in the run-up to

167

Christmas, it seemed a different world here, where green moss clung to the blackened walls, and old crisp packets and food wrappers swirled in the wind until being caught in doorways. Old grey cobbles dipped in the centre of the alley, guiding a thin brown sludge down the middle and into a rusty drain cover. This evening frost sparkled jewel-like on the rubbish and the skeletal remains of the last few brown leaves, and a thin covering of ice shone where the light from the single street lamp reached the stones.

Jean had brought along the chicken soup she'd made earlier, in Herbie's two old green thermos flasks, and some plastic bowls and spoons in a red-striped carrier bag. She quite looked forward to a natter with her boys and girls, as she thought of them. Davy, his curly hair escaping from a woollen cap that looked a couple of sizes too small, sat up from his cardboard bed, and gratefully took the bowl that Jean offered.

'A cold one tonight,' Jean stated.

'Aye,' Davy replied, tucking the red tartan blanket that she had given him the previous night around his legs. 'Least I'm still 'ere – not like poor ol' Tom.'

Jean stopped pouring the soup and peered round at the few others waiting, searching for Tom's familiar bearded face, with blue eyes that still twinkled, despite what life had thrown at him. She realised, now that he wasn't here, that she had been looking forward to seeing him. Jean clutched a wrinkled hand to her collar.

168

'What's happened?' she asked, afraid of the answer.

'Taken away in an ambulance earlier he was. I said that cough'd be the death of 'im. One of the shop staff must've seen 'im and called 'em – all sirens an' flashy lights down 'ere it was. Dunno where little Angel is though. P'raps they took 'er wiv 'em.'

'I'll ring the hospital when I get home,' Jean promised.

Jean finished dishing out the rest of the soup as quickly as she could, and was collecting up the bowls to put in her recycling bag at home when she felt she was being watched. She glanced towards the end of the alley, where a pile of wooden pallets had been stacked and, as she looked, she saw a flash of reflection in the shadow. Pouring the last dregs of soup into a bowl, Jean crept as carefully as her old legs could carry her towards the shadows. She didn't want to get too close and frighten the little dog that she could now see cowering behind the boards, and she bent slowly, holding the plastic bowl in front of her.

'Come on girl,' she whispered, 'come here.'

A little black nose appeared, followed by a small tan body, the hair matted in places, her tail wagging hesitantly. Her tatty collar, pink at one time, hung around her thin neck. Jean placed the bowl on the ground and as the little dog started to lap up the soup, Jean managed to get a hold of her tatty collar, noticing the small brass angel hanging from the buckle. 'Now I know where you got your name,' she whispered, picking her up and tucking her into her coat as best she could against the cold.

Jean collected her things together and nodded to Davy. 'I'll take care of Angel, and I'll let you know what I find out about Tom,' she promised.

Once home, Jean wasted no time, putting down a bowl of water and a saucer of left-over steak pie filling for the dog, promising she would get a bath later. She sat herself down on the worn, red velvet cushioned telephone seat and dialled the number for the local hospital. It took a few minutes before the phone was answered.

'I'm calling for information about a man brought in to hospital by ambulance earlier today,' Jean began.

'Are you a relative?' the receptionist asked.

'Well, no, but I am a friend, and he hasn't too many of those,' she replied.

'I'm sorry, but I can't give out information to anyone other than relatives.'

'He hasn't got any relatives, he's homeless. I take him food and blankets, so I'm probably the closest he has to family, and I really need to know if Tom's alright.' Jean stifled a sob.

'Ah, yes – hold on, I won't keep you a moment.'

Beethoven's Fifth started playing down the phone while Jean waited. Angel had licked the saucer clean and wandered into the hall. Jean bent to stroke the

170

terrier's ears.

'Hello?' The receptionist was back.

'Yes, I'm here.'

'I just had to check whether I could give you the information, and find out what's happened. We did have an ambulance admission earlier, a homeless man – Tom, you say?'

Jean murmured her agreement.

'Yes, well, he's been admitted to the Taylor Gordon ward. Looks to be pneumonia, but the nurses have cleaned him up and given him antibiotics, and he's a lot more comfortable than when he first came in. Still a bit touch and go though, as these things can be.'

Jean asked about visiting hours and thanked the woman, promising to go along the next day. She went back to the kitchen and put some bread on the grill and cut the cheese ready, then sat on the kitchen chair to wait.

She woke with a start. Angel was barking and pawing her leg. 'Whatever's the matter?' she asked, only then seeing the flames coming from the grill pan. 'Oh my!' she exclaimed, jumping up and turning the gas off. She ran a tea towel under the tap and placed it over her burnt supper. 'Oh, my guardian Angel,' she said, stroking the little dog. 'You certainly looked out for me today.'

Jean visited the hospital the next day, and the next, in fact she went every day for the next two weeks. She told Tom about how his dog had saved her, and heard the story of his life, of being unable to cope with losing his wife, then his job and house. They reminisced about the war, and put the world to rights, until the doctors advised that he was ready to leave. They couldn't keep him any longer, what with Christmas the following week, and needing the beds.

'Come home with me, Tom,' Jean asked, 'I've really enjoyed our chats, and I can't bear to think of you back on the streets. And there's little Angel to think about – she's settled really well. I've got the spare room and the company would be lovely.'

Christmas was not a lonely affair that year and Jean and Tom agreed that their personal Angel was better than the one at the top of the tree.

Beyond Coventry

Lois Maulkin

It's drizzly now, and I've had to wind down the window an inch to stop the car steaming up. I could flick the wipers on to clear the windscreen, but it's probably better if I don't. I'm less visible if the windows are all splattered. He knows I'm here – he watches me from that dark upstairs window when he gets a chance – but I don't want her to know I'm here, for his sake. His name's a magic trick I use on myself. I say it out loud and a tiny fire bomb shudders through me.

I'm in this for the long haul, of course. People say that if someone really loves you, they'll always be there for you. Well, that's me. I really love him and I'll always, always be there for him. Not just tonight, actually physically sitting here outside his house but always. He can depend on me. He's in there, knowing I'm outside, steadfast and reliable, not intruding. I don't need to intrude. We both know the score.

On the pavement, people hurry past every now and then. Laughing, shouting 'Happy New Year' to each other. All dressed up, heels and sparkly handbags. Raincoats and umbrellas flapping. One day he and I will be out and about like them. He'll look at me and tell me I'm beautiful and then he won't be able to hold himself back any more. He'll push me against a wall and hold me there and he'll tear off my frock with his big policeman's hands and tell me he loves me and he'll be kissing my face and we'll both be laughing and crying and...oh...it will be perfect. One day. Possibly very soon.

Funny how raindrops wriggle down a car window, isn't it? Tears run straight down your face, but rain's different. Maybe tears are heavier, because of the salt in them. Or maybe it's because glass and skin are different. Imagine having a glass face. Or a china face. Like a china doll with an expression painted on. You'd always look happy. I'm a bit like that, I think – I always look happy, I mean. I'm not made of china, obviously. Ha! That would be ridiculous. And obviously my face isn't made of glass, because my tears run straight down.

There's still no light on at that upstairs window. He hasn't put it on all evening. It's to show me he knows I'm there and he knows he can have absolute faith in me. It's how I know he loves me.

I've brought a book with me to read through the evening, which was silly really as I can't put the light on. I'm supposed to be waiting quietly in the dark, not all lit up like a Christmas tree. I've also brought a bottle of champagne and two glasses, because it might happen tonight. It could well happen. People do make big changes on New Year's Eve. He could be there now, sitting opposite her at a table in the kitchen or some other room. At the back of the house anyway, they're not in one of the rooms at the front, the whole front of the house is in darkness. He's done that for me, bless him. And he'll have both her hands in his and he'll be saying, 'Gemma, it's no good, I'm in love with someone else. I've been in love with her for a long time now. Since before I met you. You and me, Gemma, well, we're over. I don't want to be married to you any more, and we can never see each other again. When I met her it was like an angel came into my life and opened my heart and climbed inside and lives there now and I'm so happy to have her there, Gemma. I've waited six years for the feeling to go away, but it hasn't and I know it never will.'

I'm leaning back in the car seat – I've reclined it, he'd want me to be as comfortable as I can be in the circumstances – and I'm picturing the scene. She's a vile, heartless bitch and I know he wants to cut her disgusting face to pieces. I know he feels like that, because that's how I feel. She'll feel no sadness when he tells her it's over, but she'll try to stop him leaving her, purely out of spite. And all his training will come in, his negotiating skills, the psychology courses, interrogation techniques, years of forcing people to yield to his will, and he'll talk things right. He'll be doing it now. At midnight, he'll come running out to the car, and he'll jump in and shout, 'Drive, drive!' and we'll shoot off into the new year, our new life, together. I make sure the passenger door isn't locked and the key's in the ignition.

That book I brought, it's from my Mallory Towers box set. I smell the dusty edge and I'm back in my grandad's loft, running his trains. 'Has she turned up yet, Grandad?' I ask. We are talking about the little lady in the yellow coat who for years sat alone on a platform bench. Some months back I'd posted her into one of the engines, thinking she'd probably enjoy a ride. She'd not been seen since. I imagined her, deep in the bowels of the Mallard or the Sir Nigel Gresley, rolling and groaning in the plastic coals in the firebox, her OO gauge agony eternal as again and again she circles round under the eaves.

Lovely how that smell brought back that memory of Grandad's trains. I'd been reading that book before I went up the loft ladder. Darrell Rivers and her friends had just sent a classmate to Coventry. I asked Grandad what Coventry was like. He sighed and told me his Coventry stories – he pronounced it *Cuventry* – the medieval town and the cathedral and the bombings and afterwards the firestorms on Dresden. I wondered what Darrell Rivers' classmate was supposed to be doing there, and how they trusted her to get off the train at Coventry, and not go beyond, to Leamington perhaps. I pictured her, tiny in her plaits and brown pinafore, picking her solitary way across acres of smoking rubble, face turned up to see the planes flying out to bomb

176

Dresden. Strange punishment for pinching someone's tuck, I thought. Still, it might make you think twice in future.

I open my eyes and check my phone. I'm afraid I may have dozed off and feel a spasm of panic – oh my God to miss it! After all this time, to miss the moment when he comes running out looking for me. To miss him because I'm asleep. For him to think I'm not there, that I don't care about him – the thought clasps a cold hand round my heart. But no, it can't have happened yet, it's 11.03. He'll wait till midnight. Till the new year. That will be right. I put the seat upright.

There was a woman who had studied Enid Blyton books so closely that she could tell where in the stories the author had broken off writing to have her lunch. I've read a lot of Enid Blyton and I've actively looked for signs of imminent sandwiches or bowls of soup hanging over her, but I've never seen any. Mind you, I'm not very good at signs, really. I remember years ago when I thought Barry was having an affair, how angry he was when I asked him. Funny how wrong you can get things. It was the lipstick in the bed, you see. I couldn't for the life of me work out why else that lipstick had been in the bed. I used to ask Barry over and over again why I felt so rejected and unhappy. Why I cried at the dinner table and he never noticed, and just carried on eating his dinner.

'I feel,' I said once, 'as though you don't love me

any more.' I didn't mean to but I slammed the dishwasher door shut and heard the glasses chinking inside. I think one or two shattered, but I don't remember if that was that time or another.

'That's just your perception,' Barry said, walking out of the kitchen. He always used to say everything was my perception. He'd say, 'It's in your head.' By the time I'd wiped the stove, he was asleep on the settee. It was seven in the evening. I sat on a chair in the dark and watched the rain running down the window.

It's ten past eleven. My legs are feeling a bit stiff so I flap my feet round at the ankles. I'll take off my stilettos for a while as I can feel pins and needles coming on, but I'll set my alarm for ten to twelve to remind myself to put them on and be all ready for midnight. I know it wouldn't matter what I was wearing – he'd still love the very bones of me if I was wearing a bin bag – but I've made an effort. If tonight's going to be the night, I don't want to be wondering if I've got visible ear wax while he's holding me down on the bed, roaring into me, so I've been plucking and scrubbing and soaping and rinsing and waxing and tinting and moisturising and filing and buffing and shaving those bits he likes a lady to shave, I've been doing that all day to be prepared, just in case. I took a day off work to do it. And I've got black lace stockings on. Cost an absolute fortune but I know what I want him to see when it happens. He used to tell me, back in that other time, the contact phase when we texted, what he'd like to see me in. He used to ask me what I was wearing, what I was doing that day, what I'd had for lunch. He told me he'd seen Dodi Fayed's car in the warehouse where it's kept, that he'd had a row with his brother-in-law about moving a fridge, that he drank milk with his dinner, that he could be with me in under an hour to buy me coffee and a lemon muffin at any time – all I had to do was say the word. I never did, of course. I was a married woman. There was Barry to think about.

Thirst is a funny thing, isn't it? They say by the time you feel thirsty, it's too late. You should have had a drink earlier. But who gets a drink when they're not thirsty? It's about planning ahead, I suppose.

One Christmas Eve I asked Barry to mind the children so I could do the Christmas grocery shop without them. That kind of shopping's hell if you have the children with you. The supermarket was a snarling nightmare of fraught shoppers, and it took hours to get round, but I got the turkey and the potatoes and the oil and the sprouts and the pudding, the cream, the wine and the beer, the cheese and the crackers, the cranberry sauce. Then I paid, got the trolley to the car, and opened the boot to put it all in. But the boot was full. There were carrier bags of turkey and sprouts and oil and pudding and I put my shopping on the back seat. I drove home feeling I was in a dream and must suddenly wake up, and when I got home, I looked at Barry, and he said,

'I, er, I meant to say, I got the Christmas groceries yesterday.'

I stood in the hall blinking hard for a while. 'There's something very wrong with us,' I said eventually. 'Why don't we talk any more?'

'That's just your perception,' he said, slamming out to work.

The contact phase, that's my name for the first two years. He came to take a statement from me about a friend whose drink had been spiked. He walked into my life, out of the blue, and changed everything. Now I'm singing that Fern Kinney song, but my voice sounds far too loud in the quiet night and my teeth are chattering so I don't persevere.

Anyway, he texted me two days after he'd taken my statement to say he couldn't stop thinking about me and would I like to meet him for a coffee and a muffin. I knew that replying would mean that nothing would be the same again, I replied anyway, to tell him no. And I was right. He said such beautiful things. And I needed to hear them. Like sipping sea water when you are adrift in a life boat, I knew it was wrong but I just couldn't help it. Each text was a grenade of bliss and guilt. He said once, 'I am a simple man and I don't know why, but I've got to have you in my life for a long time.' It made me cry. It was the most beautiful thing anyone had said to me for years and years. I won't say he begged me, he didn't, but he made me feel like petals were opening up inside me, like my heart was filling with sunshine. Queen of the arm's length relationship, that's me. I held him off for two years. Then he stopped texting.

I cried for months on the inside, but on the outside the china face was still smiling away – I couldn't cry about it in front of Barry, could I? What would I say if he asked what the matter was? But then I'd cry over other things – like when Barry went to New York without me and brought me back a fridge magnet – and he never asked what I was upset about then, so maybe I could have done after all.

So, that was the contact phase, when we were talking and texting. Then the transition phase, when he obviously found it far too painful to text and talk and want and never to get and just couldn't bear to carry on. I texted him, of course, but he didn't reply, poor love. This was when I moved through the empty days like a blank and smiling sleepwalker.

And then came my steadfast phase. A time of grim and joyful acceptance that it was my turn to want and not have, my turn to wait. And I would bear it unendingly for him. Citalapram in hand I would be there for him, year after year, forsaking all others...

Looks like the rain's stopped. It's eleven thirty and I'm really stiffening up. Wishing I hadn't put on all this tight, strappy underwear – it's incredibly uncomfortable to sit still in that kind of kit all this time. When you think about it, it was probably designed to be taken off as quickly as possible. That's pretty much the idea of it, surely. Not to sit in a car all night, trussed up and on your own. It occurs to me I'm in the same position as the tiny lady perched on an LNER station platform bench. What's it been now, five hours? Must be. I'm not quite sure what time I got here. No one's come in or out of the house all evening. Shall I unclip some clips and loosen my corset? No, best not. I don't want him to find me unprepared. I'll lean forward over the steering wheel. Perhaps a different angle will help ease things a bit. For a while, during the transition phase, I wondered if Barry was right, if there was a problem in my head.

I wonder what Barry and the children are doing. What do the children look like now? I often think of them, but the texts had been the one thing that made my life with Barry bearable, and once they stopped there was nothing to hold on to and I put on my yellow coat and ran away on my credit card at full speed up the West Coast mainline. I went to Coventry. I phoned Barry after a fortnight, telling him I wanted custody of the children and he said he'd made sure I'd never them again; that he'd known all along I was not right in the head.

He said he was sorry he'd ever broken things off with Julie, the woman he'd been having an affair with until I found her lipstick all those years ago and he'd panicked and given her the elbow. And thinking he'd say something to give himself away, he'd stopped talking to me. At point, that very moment, I'd asked if he was seeing someone else, he stopped communicating, except little clipped lines like, 'What time's tea?', 'Is my work shirt clean?' and 'It's just your perception.' All those years of the silent treatment, punishing me for something he'd done.

My alarm wakes me. I sit up and feel momentarily dizzy, and then I remember what's going on. Just a few more minutes and a new year and, all being well, a new life, will begin. No lights on. He knows I'm still here, then. He knows what's about to happen. I squeeze my icy feet into my shoes. My hand is shaking as I apply more lipstick (it's actually Julie's – cheeky of me, but I do like irony) and check my hair in the rear view mirror. I'm obscenely excited and I can feel myself blushing.

Each minute takes a century to pass. I'm gripping the steering wheel so tightly my finger nails cut into my palms. The clock on my phone counts slowly but my heart is going like a train. The little old lady eventually came spilling out during a derailment. Her seated pose made her seem to lie there in a curl of unbearable pain between the metal rails. The steering wheel is shaking. We propped her up again on her station platform bench and she looked perfectly fine. Crying on the inside. Ready to carry on as though nothing had happened.

Two seconds to go. I'm beyond Coventry. The sky lights up.

Burns Night At The Golf Club

Barbara Sleap

They're piping in the haggis and singing Rabbie's praise,
They're mashing neeps and tatties while in a drunken haze.
It can't be any other night, it can only be the one,
To celebrate a poet and with it have some fun.

The members of the golf club are killing, 'Red, Red Rose',
And those who've had a whisky can't remember how it goes.
The captain's selling tickets for the raffle, with a kiss,
And the ladies are all wishing that they'd given this a miss.

The haggis has been toasted, with a long and drawn out ode,
The piper's cheeks are puffing, I think he might explode.
The ladies in the kitchen are looking hot and gruff,
And men in kilts queue up with plates, just hoping there's
enough.

The bagpipes keep on wailing, while everyone tucks in,
I hope it stops before the quiz, oh blimey what a din!
A toast to the lassies is next on the list, the ladies then reply,
The piper had to stop for this and everyone gives a sigh.

The songs and poems have been sung, the whisky has been downed,
But hark, I hear a distant noise, what is that groaning sound?
It isn't the rousing 'Auld Lang Syne' or 'Scotland the Brave',
'Tis the sound of poor old Robbie Burns turning in his grave.

Three Little Words

Kim Kimber

'I love you,' you said, 'marry me.'

'Yes,' I replied as if this was a normal, everyday thing to do after so short a time together. 'Yes, yes, yes!'

Family and friends smiled their congratulations but I could see they thought that it was foolish, that two months was too soon to make such a big commitment, not long enough to really know someone.

'I love you,' you said. 'Who cares what other people think?'

With hindsight, it was reckless but I knew that I wanted to be with you, 'till death do us part' and all that. The young are blessed with the ability not to think too far in the future, to the unfilled days ahead and what the consequences of their actions might be so we ignored other people's misgivings.

'Let's do it on Valentine's Day,' you said.

'Perfect!' I replied.

My mum sighed and tutted. 'It's too soon, love,' she said. 'Are you sure?'

'Yes, of course,' I laughed. 'Don't worry so much.'

Mum changed tack. 'Six weeks isn't long enough to

plan a wedding,' she said, listing all the practical difficulties and obstacles to be overcome, hoping that in the time it took to plan my big day we would change our minds. But I saw through that one.

Mum pressed on. 'There's really not enough time to organise everything...'

Oh, but there was. Maybe not the kind of wedding that she had always imagined for her only daughter with me dressed in a frothy, meringue dress with a price tag that could feed the homeless for a year. With rows of smiling bridesmaids and, of course, the mother of the bride in a garish new outfit topped off with a ridiculous feathered hat that made her resemble a peacock.

Not that kind of wedding. But a day where the bride wore a hastily purchased dress from a charity shop (slightly on the loose side, once white satin) and the groom looked nervous in a borrowed suit and mismatching socks under holey shoes. With a reception in the local pub and a wedding breakfast of crisps and beer. There was more than enough time to arrange a marriage of that kind.

No one said anything to my face but I knew what they were thinking; it will end badly.

'Ignore the doubters,' you said, squeezing my hand. 'I love you.'

So, on 14th February we were married.

In the end my parents and siblings, aunts and uncles rallied round as families do. My mum and dad knew, better than my future husband, how headstrong I could be and they hid their concern behind forced smiles as they toasted the bride and groom.

It wasn't a large wedding; the short notice and lack of planning took care of that. But my family were there along with my husband's last foster parents. The absence of many guests on the groom's side was a little strange but I knew that he came from a broken home and had had a troubled childhood, uprooted from one place to another, so it wasn't really that odd at all when you came to think about it!

I was marrying an orphan, abandoned and alone – it appealed to the heroine in me.

I heard them whispering though, my relations and friends, and caught snatches of sentences here and there, 'psychiatric care', 'not long out of hospital', 'keep a close eye'. I didn't care; my new husband and I had no secrets, well, not many anyway.

Valentine's Day, the most romantic night of the year and I was a new bride. The best day of my life.

'Now, you're mine,' you said as we snuggled close together drinking champagne, courtesy of my parents, in the uncomfortable double bed upstairs in the pub where a few hours earlier we had been celebrating our marriage.

'Always,' I replied as we clinked our glasses, naively unaware of the hidden horrors that can be contained in three little words.

'I love you,' you said.

But jealousy is a terrible emotion that sneaks up like a green creeper and winds itself around the heart. It started with small things; the excessive questioning, 'Where are you going? Who are you meeting? What time will you be home?'

It quickly developed into obsession and what could be described as 'stalking'. If you can 'stalk' someone you are married to, the police didn't seem to think so. It wasn't even as if there was good reason to be suspicious but the monster, once released, was like a viper poisoning our relationship.

Then came the restrictions; no more drinks after work, no nights out with friends, trips to the gym... The 'rules' were handwritten on pieces of card and pasted over the walls of the kitchen like badly applied wallpaper.

Come home straight after work

No talking to people you don't know

No going out

No messaging friends on Facebook

No flirting

No, no, no...

The list grew longer and fear increased. How can someone so loving and caring become possessive and controlling in such a short time? *Marry in haste*, they say, *repent at leisure*.

If I hadn't rushed into marriage so quickly, if I

hadn't ignore my parents' misgivings, if I hadn't been so determined to prove everyone wrong, I would have admitted that I needed help and gone home, that this was too big for me to deal with on my own. But pride and love, yes love, in spite of the now frequent slaps and bruises, made me stay even though I knew that it was becoming dangerous.

And then would come 'sorry' and 'it won't happen again' until the next time, both of us clinging on to the merry-go-round of our toxic relationship, neither one of us able or willing to let go.

We managed a year, then on our first wedding anniversary, Valentine's Day, things got out of control. It started as a silly argument about how we should celebrate, of all things. How daft! But we shouted, slapped and swore.

Memories of the many previous fights that had punctured the first year of our marriage, like arrows on a dartboard, fuelled the rage. All the spiteful, hurtful comments, things that couldn't be unsaid, echoed in our minds, stoking the rage that burned hot like coals.

You are much bigger than me, and stronger. I knew that it would hurt, really hurt, if you ever decided to punch me. But you didn't and wouldn't, ever. After all, you loved me. But you should have listened to the warnings of those who knew when they said that getting married was a mistake...

As the knife drops from my hand, I feel no remorse.

Psychopaths don't, so my psychiatrist said, and I feel elated as I watch you twitch and writhe in pain on the kitchen floor, wheezing your last breath.

'Now, you're mine,' I say. 'Happy Valentine's Day, I love you.'

Valentine's Day In New York

Josephine Gibson

Sarah removed her economy class headphones, switched off the film and, resting her head back, closed her eyes. The drone of the jet engines had meant she couldn't hear the dialogue very well, despite having turned the volume to full. It actually felt a relief to be shut in an aeroplane for eight hours with no one to make any demands on her and it finally meant she had time to think.

It had been a busy half-term with the usual post-Christmas tummy bugs and flu spreading through the school. With a strong stomach and lengthy years in teaching Sarah was immune to most viruses; but inevitably the staff absences had led to long hours and late nights at a time when she would really prefer to be focusing on her private life.

'This is what it's like, dating a teacher,' she'd laughed with Ray, in an empty Indian restaurant at 10.30pm on a Thursday night. 'You never see them, and when you do, they're comatose with their head in a bowl of biryani.'

'Well, I've got a plan,' Ray replied, lightly stroking her hand with his little finger. 'How about coming to visit me in New York for half-term?'

Sitting in the plane, Sarah smiled to herself. This was something she liked about him: he didn't complain but instead presented her with a fully-formed plan and would accept no excuses. When she'd protested about her work commitments he'd challenged her to speak to her staff who were unanimous in their opinion that she should definitely go, have fun, and forget about school for a week.

Of course, they couldn't possibly know the real reason for her reluctance, and neither did Ray. She sighed. It was a wonderful opportunity – to go out and meet him while he was there on business – the only cost the price of her economy flight and a few dollars for sightseeing. She felt like a lovesick teenager because she wanted to spend every waking moment with him. She just wasn't sure about the sleeping moments.

He had put her under no pressure – she'd felt a charge of energy when he'd talked about them sharing his hotel room that later converted into a passionate embrace when they'd said goodbye. She'd felt sure, confident, knowing. Perhaps she had been slightly drunk? As she watched the progress of the plane on the information screen, the inexorable swallowing of the miles, she wondered how she'd allowed herself to be persuaded.

She now doubted the wisdom of a grand, romantic gesture and a wave of longing washed over her as she remembered her first night with Peter in a narrow student bed. The room was as freezing as only an old stone, medieval, last-bastion of the male Oxford College, could be. It had been a joyful experience to feel the warmth of his naked skin against hers as they playfully fought for a larger share of the duvet, culminating in that glorious moment when she'd felt him hard inside her and she'd pressed against him, slid herself against him, wanting more and more.

So many moments, so many years of loving that man, and then having to tend to his poor, wasted body, emaciated and finally cold for ever. She felt her tears wet on her cheeks and leant forward, both to hide them and search for a tissue from her handbag. How did you ever get over your husband dying in the prime of life? What was she thinking? What the hell was she doing, flying to New York? She wanted to turn the bloody plane around and get off.

*****

'Good morning, beautiful.' Ray kissed her on the cheek and, leaning over her, laid a single red rose on the pillow in front of her. 'Happy Valentine's Day.'

'Oh Ray,' she said, turning on to her back, 'where did you hide that?'

She'd conducted a thorough investigation of their hotel room when she'd arrived, unpacking her clothes and organising his, tidying his toiletries, inspecting the contents of the mini bar, and opening the drawers to see what perks an executive room included. There had been no rose last night.

'I have ways and means,' he replied, archly, 'or shall we say, an accommodation with the bell boy. Delivered this morning.'

'Well, I'm not so organised, but I do have a card.' Sitting up, she swung her legs out of bed and, back towards him, reached down for her hotel dressing gown. She tied it tightly around her before standing up. 'Could you open the curtains?'

He pressed a button next to the bed and, with a motorised whirring sound, the full length curtains opened to reveal the lower Manhattan skyline. Standing in front of the floor-to-ceiling windows she looked out. The new World Trade Centre building glinted, its angled windows reflecting the early morning sunshine, the sky a clear blue. Looking down she could see plumes of condensation from the buildings below them. It was obviously very cold outside.

'What a fantastic view,' she breathed.

'Indeed,' said Ray, and he looked directly at her, 'I'm enjoying it very much. But do we need the dressing gown?'

'Ray! We haven't got time for that! We've got a lot of sightseeing to do. I'm so looking forward to seeing it all. I tell you what – I'll use the bathroom first, shall I?'

Flustered, she crossed the room to the en suite, shutting the door resolutely behind her, forgetting the Valentine's card.

Despite it being the coldest Valentine's Day in New York for one hundred years, with TV warnings about not venturing outside, they joined throngs of other tourists to visit the highlights of New York. Sarah felt like a child again, giddy with excitement, cheerful despite the many security checks as they visited the Statue of Liberty by boat, navigated the labyrinthine subway system to Times Square, route-marched their way through the grid of streets to the Intrepid Air, Sea and Space Museum (not Sarah's choice, but essential for Ray), and after a quick burger, flew up in an elevator to the Top of the Rock. By now it was dark and it was magical to see the lights in the streets below them, and the skyscrapers illuminated by their many windows.

'I think this is what is called a "peak experience",' she laughed, as she cuddled up to Ray, trying to use him as a shield against the bitter wind, 'but it's freezing! Can we go inside now?'

She was beginning to flag. The time difference was catching up with her, and although it was barely 8.00pm, her body was telling her it was past midnight. It seemed a perfect excuse, and after they hailed a yellow cab to take them back to the hotel, she fell asleep on Ray's shoulder and missed most of the journey home. Ray made no comment when she came out of the bathroom in her pyjamas with her teeth brushed and he didn't seem to mind when she said goodnight. He kissed her and asked if the hockey on TV was disturbing her. She was already asleep.

It was 4.00am New York time when she woke up. She lay in the dark, listening to Ray's quiet breathing. It was a long time since she'd shared a bed with someone and she luxuriated in his body heat. She felt absurdly glad that he didn't snore. She reached out and ran her hand down his hip, noticing he was still wearing his boxers. The sound of his breathing stopped – he was instantly awake. He turned towards her. Neither of them spoke as they moved closer together and began to kiss. Words were unnecessary. This was life. Her breathing shortened. She wanted him. Fiercely. Like she'd never wanted anyone before.

Afterwards, all was quiet. They lay, spooned together, his arm around her, his head buried against her neck. She began to weep, silently, and a fragment of a long ago read sentence came to mind. Perhaps it was Shakespeare – or maybe the Bible?

'For love is as strong as death.'

Sarah slept.

Februaryness

Lois Maulkin

'I've never really taken to February,' he was saying as he sat at the table, picking little pieces of shell off his boiled egg.

She was buttering toast. Testy. 'What are you talking about?'

'February.' He sighed and dipped his teaspoon in.

'What about February?'

He looked darkly at her. 'The Februaryness of it. Imbolc. Lupercalia.'

'Clap-trap,' she snapped.

When he'd finished his breakfast, he started to push the spoon through the bottom of the eggshell. It was something he'd always done, ever since he was a little boy. It made sure witches could not row out to sea in it to brew up storms. It made a mess in the bottom of the egg cup. It made her say, 'For God's sake, don't do that.'

'You'll regret it if I don't.'

He scraped back his chair and went out to get the paper.

She cleared the table, tutting. His egg cup was

empty.

She waited in the front room for him to come back, standing sideways at the window, arms folded and looking over her shoulder up the road, tapping her foot.

*****

The shop bell pinged as he went in. There was a shaft of sunlight lazing over the fat weekend papers on the counter and dust motes swam slowly up and down in it. The girl at the till asked if he wanted any Valentine's cards, and he said no, he certainly did not, thank you very much, paid for his paper and went out. He almost turned towards home, but seemed to remember something and went the other way instead.

Twenty minutes later, still at the window, she was angry. Forty minutes later, she was livid. Two hours later, still at the window, she was trembling with fury. She buttoned her blue coat firmly to the neck and knotted her scarf viciously. She was taking no more nonsense. It was nearly lunchtime. It was beyond belief.

Marching up to the shop counter she felt momentarily that she must be dreaming but she banged the flat of her hand down and hissed, 'Who was he with when he left the shop? I take it he did leave the shop?'

The girl at the till said, 'Well, yes, he did but I didn't see anyone–'

Stamping back down the road she quivered with

rage. Her neighbour answered his front door as she pounded it with the side of her fist. She said, 'We'll need to go in your car if we're to catch them.'

He looked blankly at her. 'I'm sorry?'

She clenched and unclenched her hands and rolled her eyes.

'Your car, man. Quickly. Come on.' She leaned forward. The tip of her nose touched the tip of his and he stepped backwards. 'It's an emergency.'

He picked up his keys from the hall table and slipped his coat over his pyjamas. She was looking up and down the road, crying, 'Where's your car? Where is it?'

'What's the matter? Are you ill?'

'No, I'm not. For God's sake, where's your car?'

The engine started at the third attempt.

'Down past the paper shop and just keep going,' she said grimly.

The town was cold and silent as they drove out along the coast road. The sun glinted off the windscreen.

'He's gone off with some ruddy tart,' she spat.

'Really?' said the neighbour. 'I mean, *really*?'

She turned to look at him. 'He doesn't know when he's well off, that's his trouble.'

Miles passed. She stared ahead as they neared the coast. 'You can stop at the harbour.'

Gulls were blowing about in the chilly sunshine and grey waves smacked and sucked at the sea wall which she scrambled up and strode along, bent into the wind, scanning out over the water.

'There!' she shouted.

The neighbour, wondering how his slippers would cope with this quantity of cold salt water, pulled his overcoat more tightly round and looked where she was pointing.

'Is it a buoy?' he asked presently.

A round, fragile looking, white craft bobbed and turned on the water, gliding past the small wooden boats which rode at anchor.

'Is it a...a...big tea cup? From a fairground?' asked the neighbour.

'It's his bloody eggshell,' she said.

It was just possible to see two figures sitting inside. A man reading a newspaper and a bony woman, dressed in black, her hair blowing like weeds into the sky, rowing steadily out to sea.

A Love Story

Sue Duggans

It was cold. Joe walked with purpose down the High Road which was bustling with people toing and froing as they went about their business before returning home. The road was particularly busy and a driver sounded his horn repeatedly as he waited impatiently for a delivery van to move on.

Joe's thin jacket barely kept out the cold and his ears and nose tingled. His hands were thrust deep in his pockets partly to keep them warm and, more importantly, so that he could feel the small box. Its surface was smooth and Joe ran his thumb over it time and again. He couldn't wait to be able to present it. A little shiver of excited expectation ran down his spine.

When Joe turned the corner of Bentley Road he stopped for a moment to gaze into the beautifully-dressed window of 'Petra's Posies'. Petra had run the florists here for as long as he could remember and she was often standing in the doorway smiling at passers-by. Today, Valentine's Day, the shop looked impressive – buckets of flowers stood in rows on the pavement outside and the window display was jam-packed with flowers, balloons and bows. Money was tight but, one day, Joe would walk away with the biggest bouquet he could carry. One day.

For the time being the box and its contents, nestled in his pocket, preoccupied Joe's thoughts. He held it and could feel the minute brass catch with the tiniest of screws which kept it firmly closed. It served a practical purpose but was a feature of the box too. He walked on. Six or seven minutes more and he'd be there. The cold was worrying him less now.

*****

It was a special day. Helen was dashing around tidying the little flat which she shared with Joe. She washed the cereal bowls left in the sink from breakfast and made sure that dinner was nearly done. Joe would be home in no time. She peeped through the nets to see if she could catch sight of him coming down the road then looked at the photo of the two of them together last Christmas. Joe was wearing one of those flimsy tissue hats from the Christmas cracker and a big smile. Money was tight and there would be no going out to the cinema or fancy restaurants for some time. *One day*, she thought.

Helen had made a shepherd's pie, Joe's favourite.

The doorbell rang and when Helen opened it the bright streetlight silhouetted Joe's slight frame.

'Hello darling!' she greeted him fondly and he

stepped inside, one hand still firmly in his pocket. Helen drew him to her and gave him an affectionate hug. She could smell the fresh air in his soft hair. They walked through to the small kitchen and, in an instant, Joe knew what was cooking. He smiled.

His heart filled with pride and love for the woman before him as he took the little box from his pocket.

'Happy birthday, Mum!' He handed Helen the little box with its brass catch. 'I made it in woodwork. It took me ages,' he added.

Helen opened the box and inside found a wooden bead necklace, strung on leather. The tiny beads had letters burnt on – 'I LOVE YOU'.

'Joe, it's wonderful,' she said. 'I'm the luckiest mum in the world.' She kissed him on the cheek and Joe grinned. He'd waited all day for this moment.

And the shepherd's pie was delicious!

About The Authors

Sue Duggans

Sue is a recently-retired primary school teacher and a new and very proud granny. Like many retired people, she wonders how she found time to work!

Sue enjoys travelling in the UK and spending time with family and friends, knitting, reading and, of course, writing.

Writing provides Sue with both stimulation and challenge and the writing group continues to be a source of inspiration, friendship and great fun.

Josephine Gibson

Josephine, the fourth of five children, was born in County Durham to a family dominated by animals and the country. Her family moved to rural Surrey and then to the wilds of Dartmoor where Josephine grew up.

Since leaving home she has lived in London, the Midlands, Surrey and, recently, Southend-on-Sea. Her experiences of the solitude of vast open spaces and the chaotic joy of human relationships inform her writing.

Michele Hawkins

Michele is a relatively new member of the writing group. She pondered about joining for several months but wishes she had 'bitten the bullet' earlier as the group is warm, friendly and very supportive of each other.

As her children are independent, hubbie is happy in a new job and she now works part-time, Michele has found that there is only so much housework one woman can do and decided to finally pursue other interests. In addition to the WI and writing group, Michele has recently joined the Rock Choir. No audition required – thank goodness!

To balance her hitherto hidden creative side, she regularly attends a gym. Michele believes that this makes up for her love of wine and crisps and, naturally, means that more can be consumed!

Kim Kimber

Kim is an Advanced Professional Member of the Society for Editors and Proofreaders (SfEP) and has guided many first-time authors to publication.

The former editor of a parenting magazine, Kim has had several articles published in magazines and newspapers and currently compiles quiz questions on popular culture. In 2017 Kim won *Writing Magazine*'s crime competition with her short story *Number Seven*.

Kim became a member of WoSWI in 2011 and

formed the writing group shortly afterwards. She is proud of the group's many achievements which include the publication of two anthologies, *Write On The Coast* in 2013 and *Ten Minute Tales* in 2015. Having returned to Essex from London in 2001, she now resides in Westcliff-on-Sea with her family.

Lois Maulkin

By day, manager of a local charity shop, painter and mum of four. By night, rather tired, Lois writes in her spare time.

Her work has featured in *LiveShopEatSouthend*, *Write On The Coast,* and *Ten Minute Tales,* which was *Writing Magazine's* Anthology of the Year in 2016. Lois was runner-up in the national Women's Institute Lady Denman Cup competition in 2016 for her comic take on the WI of the future.

Born and bred in Essex, Lois lives and works in Southend-on-Sea.

Pat Sibbons

Pat is one of the newest members of the group. Originally from Bermondsey, South East London, she has lived with her family in Leigh-on-Sea for the past twenty-five years.

After working for many years as a Building Control

Officer and Environmental Health Technician for various London Local Authorities, she now works part-time as a receptionist at a local yoga studio and a session worker for a young carers' charity.

In her spare time Pat enjoys yoga, gardening and cooking. She has always wanted to write and is very much enjoying being part of such a creative and warm group of women.

Barbara Sleap

Barbara is the oldest member of the group but, at seventy-two, she is still young at heart and likes to keep fit by doing aqua aerobics and T'ai Chi.

Having retired from her job as a travel consultant twelve years ago, Barbara is seldom bored, especially as she has five grandchildren to keep her busy. Her hobbies are reading, travelling, pottering in the garden and, as her husband is a keen cook, they enjoy hosting dinner parties for friends.

Barbara joined the writing group because she has always been a scribbler. 'It has been an interesting and enlightening experience,' says Barbara, 'and with Kim's expert guidance my writing now has focus. Our meetings are great fun as we all have such different styles and ideas. I look forward to further exciting challenges and much more scribbling in future.'

Trisha Todd

When Trisha joined the WI several years ago, and then the writing group, she never imagined the change it would make to her life.

Whilst working on previous anthologies Trisha found she really enjoyed proofreading, so much so that she took a recognised course, passed with Distinction and became a member of the Society for Editors and Proofreaders (SfEP).

Trisha left her job, set herself up as a freelance proofreader, and she has now worked with a large fitness chain and several authors. She says, 'It's funny how things work out sometimes.'

Westcliff-on-Sea Women's Institute

WESTCLIFF-ON-SEA
WOMEN'S INSTITUTE

(Registered Charity No. XT 36711)

From florists to bakers, teachers to full-time mums, there isn't a typical member of Westcliff-on-Sea Women's Institute (affectionately known as WoSWI). We come from all walks of life and cover all age ranges.

What we do have in common is a desire to get the most out of life. We enjoy the company of interesting women. We like to support and get involved with our community, broaden our horizons and learn new skills, as well as indulging in lots of cake and the odd tipple! We even have our own cocktail (the Hot Flush!).

Our interests include crafts (it is the WI!), culture, education, keeping fit and social activities. Since our first meeting in September 2009, hundreds of women have come along to see what WoSWI is all about, many going on to join one of our sub-groups, from cycling and walking to reading and writing, where they have made friends and taken up new hobbies.

Each year, WoSWI members vote on a local charity to support and raise money for. This year's chosen charity is Southend Mencap Operatic and Dramatic Society (MODS), and we hope to match the success of previous years in raising significant sums for such a worthy cause.

If we have piqued your interest and you would like to find out more about any aspect of WoSWI, visit our website for further details.

www.westcliffwi.co.uk

MODS Drama Group

(Registered Charity No. 1078686)

Mencap Operatic and Dramatic Society (MODS) is an amazing group of people based in Southend-on-Sea, Essex.

The weekly drama group is run by Andrew and Georgie Watson for adults with disabilities and, with the help of dedicated volunteers, they support the members in learning their individual roles for the annual MODS show. They write, produce, choreograph, and direct every single show, ensuring that each and every member is able to perform to the best of their abilities.

The first MODS performance, *Gunshots and Golden Garters*, was staged in 2006 and since then the group has put on an incredible twelve further shows. Over the years, the group has performed a wide range of completely original musicals, featuring fabulous music and wonderful songs.

MODS productions originally took place at The

Eastwood School Theatre and they have appeared twice at the Cliffs Pavilion but more recent shows have been held at the historic Palace Theatre in Westcliff-on-Sea.

The drama group continues to be extremely popular with over fifty members performing in the latest show to packed audiences. Anyone interested in finding out more, or in joining MODS, should apply either to Southend Mencap or visit MODS Southend Mencap Facebook page which is updated weekly.

www.southendmencap.org.uk/mods-drama-group

Also by
WoSWI Writing Group

Ten Minute Tales

Write On The Coast

If you have enjoyed our books
please be kind enough to review us on
Amazon

Lightning Source UK Ltd.
Milton Keynes UK
UKHW012327101118
332146UK00001B/4/P